RICHARD HOYT

WHOO?

Complete and Unabridged

LINFORD
Leicester

First published in the United States of America

First Linford Edition
published 2006

This is a work of fiction. All the characters and events portrayed in this book are fictitious, and any resemblance to real people or events is purely coincidental.

British Library CIP Data

Hoyt, Richard, *1941* –
   Whoo?.—Large print ed.—
   Linford mystery library
   1. Denson, John (Fictitious character)—Fiction
   2. Private investigators—United States— Fiction
   3. Indians of North America—Fiction
   4. Murder—Investigation—Washington (State)—
   Fiction 5. Logging—Environmental aspects—
   Washington (State)—Fiction
   6. Detective and mystery stories 7. Large type books
   I. Title
   813.5′4 [F]

ISBN 1–84617–456–2

Published by
F. A. Thorpe (Publishing)
Anstey, Leicestershire

Set by Words & Graphics Ltd.
Anstey, Leicestershire
Printed and bound in Great Britain by
T. J. International Ltd., Padstow, Cornwall

This book is printed on acid-free paper

WHOO?

When John Denson undertakes to clear a Washington State client of a marijuana charge, he finds himself in spotted owl country. He discovers that the tiny bird is up against the logging industry. A spotted owl is found murdered, and Denson's partner, Willie Prettybird, wants him to investigate. But then Jenny MacIvar of the Fish and Wildlife Service is murdered; a simple marijuana case turns into a hunt for a killer, and Denson may be the next victim.

For Doug and Wendy Gregg

The owl is below at night
when it is daylight
in the grave.

— MYTH OF THE SNOHOMISH

1

At Dusk, in the Wind

On Wednesday I was on my way to a case in Sixkiller, Washington, trying to imagine what the comely Donna Cowapoo must be like. Willie Prettybird had described Donna's many charms in direct and specific detail, Donna being an artist who lived in Portland. Since Sixkiller was only fifty or sixty miles north of Portland, Willie said, why you never knew.

Of such matters does a gumshoe think on a dark and windy afternoon.

In front of me the sun was setting, its searing reds as hot as a hooker's lipstick. Below the freeway to my right, a flock of Canadian geese, heads down, breasts puffed out against the buffeting east wind, sat huddled on a mud bar facing the last warmth of the sun.

I bought a plastic cup of coffee in Arlington to keep me awake, but the awful stuff began inflicting pain in my bladder by the time I got to the ancient Indian fishing grounds covered by the dam at The Dalles, and then I was quickly upon the town itself.

Fifteen miles later I pulled in to a rest stop in front of an overlook above Memaloose Island, where for hundreds of years Indians had left their dead above ground to meet the Great Spirit. I had seen photographs of thousands of bleached human bones piled high on Memaloose Island; the bones — once there in the sun and rain and wind and ice and snow — were now gone, all but the tip of the island covered by the reservoir of yet another dam, Bonneville.

There was hardly any traffic on the interstate and the reststop parking lot at Memaloose was empty; I parked beside a metal light pole, zipped up my coat, and pulled my Irish wool hat over the tops of my ears. I threw open the door and sprinted for the toilet, watching I didn't slip on a patch of ice.

I got back to the refuge of my VW bus and fumbled with the seat belt in the cold; a shadow floated soundlessly out of the forest and held momentarily in the yellow of the light directly in front of me. With one lazy flap of wings that was forever, it rose six inches and held once more.

An owl.

Then — as quickly and silently as it had appeared — it was gone.

Slightly unnerved and with the memory of the hovering bird vivid in my mind, I fired up the bus and shot on down the Columbia River gorge — the cold east wind hard on my ass. This was the heart of the magnificent gorge. Fir and spruce and pine rose to the high cascades on either side of the river.

As I came to the overpass that led to the Bridge of the Gods just below Bonneville, I saw a woman on the eastbound side peering into the engine of a Volvo with its hood up. The Volvo was parked just off the entrance. She threw up her hands in an aw-fuck gesture and braced herself against the wind. Her pumped-up nylon windbreaker made her look like an astronaut with blowing hair.

Two big rigs whooshed *ka-fooo! ka-fooo!* by her on their way to Pendleton, Baker, Boise, and points east.

I eased up on the accelerator and glanced back as her silhouette, a shroud in the darkness, strode to the Volvo's trunk in two long, pissed-off strides. Then I was under the overpass and she was gone, long legs and blowing hair and all.

Ah, well, I thought: One flew east; one flew west. I still had Donna Cowapoo to imagine.

I eased into the slow lane thinking the Volvo lady would be okay. With a wind like this, there'd be no problem for a woman in distress. Somebody would stop. Besides, it was several miles to the next exit where I could turn around.

My radio was on the blink, so I didn't have anything to do except drive in silence and grit my teeth when the door rattled and think about the stranded woman. Just as well the radio didn't work; it seemed like a nut-a-minute time in the news, a parade of screwballs who preyed on vulnerable women.

What if some asshole got to her?

Crap! I put the accelerator on the floor. A gust of wind caught me from the side; I held on to the steering wheel with both hands as the bus almost jumped into the other lane. The rattle of the sliding side door, worn just a microscopic tad from its original German perfection, came in short, annoying bursts, *ra-ba-ba-ba-ba*, *ra-ba-ba-ba-ba*, followed by wonderful spaces of blessed silence.

Through the din I could hear the hum of the eighteen-year-old rebuilt engine, as reassuring as a heartbeat. A Volkswagen engine was mortal in a way that the newer, high-tech engines were not. There was no shield of cooling water to mask the rattle and clatter of its innards. A Volkswagen engine forced you to listen to those pistons whipping up and down and share their joys and agonies.

After almost destroying my engine in my imagination if not in fact, it was my bet that when I got back there she would be gone, back in The Dalles eating prime rib with a handsome neurosurgeon who had stopped by in his Mercedes.

Her Volvo was still there, but where was she?

I parked my bus behind the Volvo and got out; I pulled my hat over my ears and walked up to take a look. Shit oh dear, it was cold. And that wind. Foo! I wondered how people lived in a place like this and had to laugh because I grew up here.

She was still there, sitting with her arms crossed, apparently resigned to being stuck. She had beautiful auburn hair.

I tapped on the window, and she looked up with green eyes, grateful, yet cautious as she should be. She was a good-looking woman. The top of the window came down an inch, but she kept the door locked.

'I was figuring you might need a little help,' I said.

She shivered. 'Fuckers wouldn't stop. Wind like this. What's wrong with people? My God!'

'They don't like the cold, I suppose, and there's always the possibility that some crazed man will attack them with a machete or an Uzi.'

6

She looked up at me, then back at my bus, then up at me again, obviously concluding I was okay. Just to make sure, watching me, she said, 'What've you got in that thing, ropes and donkeys? Is that why you came back? Looking for a victim?'

I shook my head earnestly. 'No, ma'am. Whips and German shepherds,' I said, trying to be as droll as I could manage. 'They're hip dogs, really. I got 'em all specially trained for women I pick up on the highway.'

I paused. She grinned. 'Oh, well then, no problem. Where in the hell have you been, anyway?'

I liked her. Maybe Willie was right. Chief Dumbshit he called me. 'Nag, nag, nag,' I said. 'I had to find a place to turn around. Thought I'd ruin my engine, but it held up. What happened to your noble hunk of metal? I thought Volvos were supposed to run forever.'

'No idea. The damn thing started making weird noises so I thought I better turn around and head back to The Dalles rather than chance not making it to

Portland. I got halfway down the ramp to the eastbound lanes when the oil light went on, so I pulled to the side of the road. Then nobody would stop. I must have been here for nearly an hour. It was zoom, zoom, zoom. Nobody even slowed.'

'On a night like this, maybe they were afraid of the Bridge of the Gods.'

She rolled her eyes, oh sure.

'I can drive you back to The Dalles, if you'd like. They've got service stations there and places to stay. You can find out what's wrong in the morning.'

She seemed uncertain.

'Or maybe you prefer Cascade Locks or Hood River. Wherever.'

She didn't want to drive off with a stranger.

'Or you can wait it out here; I can send a tow truck back if you'd like.'

She sighed. She was stuck. 'The Dalles, why not?' she said, and rolled up the window.

Backpack in hand, she trailed after me as I walked back to the bus. She said, 'What's got you traveling up this gorge in the wind?'

'Two young kids fighting a pot rap.'

'Huh?'

'I'm a private detective,' I said. 'How about you?'

'Owls.'

'What else but owls. Barn owls? Screech owls?'

'Spotted owls.'

'Oh, boy.' I shook my head and looked back at her.

She grinned. She had dimples. I liked dimples. 'What do you mean, what else but owls?'

'An owl flew out of the forest into the parking lot at Memaloose. It was spooky, right out of Poe.' I opened the door of my bus for her. 'You're lucky this is not logging country. I could have been a logger.'

She hopped up onto the seat, laughing. 'If I'd thought you were a logger, I would have stayed in my car.'

2

Recount

We got in Big Blue, and I worked the bus up through the gears to fourth, bucking a head wind that held me at fifty-five, and we shook, rattled, and nearly everything except rolled, the side door clattering with enthusiasm.

'John's my name,' I said.

'Jenny,' she said, and we shook. 'Helluva wind.' She smelled good.

'In a wind like this you sail a bus, you don't drive it.'

'You say you saw me from the other side?'

I could feel her watching me. A honking big semi clattered by with a rush. I had my hands full with the head wind, so I couldn't get a look at her face in the darkness. 'Figured you'd be gone by the time I got back, but what the hell.'

'Thank you. You said you were a private detective?'

I lifted up my hip and retrieved my wallet and slipped her a Denson and Prettybird business card with the face of a crafty coyote on the outside. The crafty coyote was drawn by the artist Donna Cowapoo who had been on my mind earlier.

'Willie Prettybird?'

'My partner. He's a full-blooded Cowlitz.'

Jenny read the card in the light of the dashboard. ''John Denson and Willie Prettybird, private investigators. Seattle and Portland. Licensed in Oregon, Washington, Idaho, Montana, and Alaska.' Say, that's impressive!'

'Actually, it should be just plain John Denson, private investigator. Willie only helps me when I have a job I can't handle by myself or have too many jobs at once.'

'Ahh, I see,' she said.

'Seattle's where I have my answering service. Willie has an apartment in northwest Portland. He likes to be able to flash a business card with his name on it.'

I grinned. 'I don't mind. People think we're a high-powered agency: a tandem of pros working the streets instead of one moron clinging by his fingernails and an Indian sidekick. Also, Willie Prettybird makes a classy addition to a card, don't you think?'

'It's not your everyday name, that's true. Are you on a job?'

'Willie's down at Brookings working on the case of the humpbacked flute player you've probably been reading about. I've got a mill worker and his wife in Washington who took a couple of weeks off to go fishing, and the day after they got back, the sheriff showed up with a search warrant, and damned if he didn't find a shack up the creek filled with drying marijuana.' I shook my head.

'Was it their pot?'

'They say not. They say they don't know how it got there.'

'And you have to come up with evidence to support them?'

'If I can find any. I'll talk to the couple Friday afternoon, then I'll know more. Working for the old Boog this time out.' I figured I might as well get it over with.

'The Boog?'

'Boogie Dewlapp.'

She looked amused. 'The guy on the tube?'

Boogie Dewlapp ran television commercials throughout Washington state and got some odd cases from people, mostly those who were poor or isolated or desperate and had never had reason to use a lawyer before and so trusted in the telephone number Boogie gave them in his pitch. He was considered a joke in fashionable, or even semifashionable, circles. His brother Olden ran an office out of Portland.

'Boogie likes me because I don't mind a little travel or working small towns. I've got fishing rods in the back. Also, I know how to read and can figure out how to turn on the Cubs.'

'In those television ads Boogie comes off as a sleaze with a heart of gold. Is that the way he is in real life?'

'Well, sort of. He hires kids fresh out of law school to try most of his cases. No experience, but they do their damnedest.'

13

'And he's got a brother in Portland.'

'Olden Dewlapp. Boogie II, I call him. Willie knows him better than me.' I wondered: was this woman married? Where was her inevitable boyfriend? Wilbert or Clarence or Harold or whatever the hell his name was. 'How about you and your owls, lady in a Volvo that poops out in the cold wind?' I liked her eyes, and there seemed no doubt that she liked mine.

Another truck zoomed by; I held on to the wheel as a wave of wind pushed my bus to one side.

She said, 'I count owls. You know anything about the spotted owl controversy?'

'Let's see if I've got this straight,' I said. 'The spotted owl is an endangered species that lives in the remaining old-growth stands of Douglas fir, and if it weren't for the fuss over saving the owls, much of that timber would already have been cut.'

'The timbermen say the real fight is about trees, but it's easier for the environmentalists to work up public sympathy for an owl. If you eliminate a forest you eliminate flying squirrels and woodpeckers too, but that doesn't make any difference. The spotted owl has became a celebrated cause. Is the owl endangered or not, and what is to be done with this timber?'

I said, 'Which timber gets the ax and which gets spared currently depends on where the owls are, I take it.'

'Where they are and how many. Not all spotted owls are endangered or in question, mind you, only the northern spotted owl, one of three subspecies of the spotted owl.'

I grinned. 'Ahh, such power doth wieldeth the mighty owl and definitions thereof.'

'But it's Bosley Ellin who likes his lawyers.'

I knew from reading the papers that Bosley Ellin was much given to filing lawsuits claiming that the owl count in Washington state's Gifford Pinchot National Forest was unaccountably low. Lawyers for the Audubon Society and the Sierra Club were on the other side of the legal quarreling, claiming the count was far too high.

The corporate lumber giants owned so much timberland they didn't need logs from national forests and so were above the fray, attempting to appear calm and civilized, even statesmanlike. The small, independent mills were the ones threatened with extinction.

I said, 'Ellin owns a mill himself, right? But that isn't why his name is in the papers all the time, is it?'

'He owns Skamania-Pacific in Sixkiller, Washington, which sits at the base of some prime Douglas fir tracts in Gifford Pinchot National Forest. That's about fifty or sixty miles north of Portland. The reason you see him quoted in the papers is because he's the chairman of the spotted owl study committee of something called the Northwest Forest Resource Council. And why is it you're grinning?'

'My client, Terry Harkenrider, drives a forklift for Skamania-Pacific.'

'Ahh, so you know something about the territory.'

16

'I know what Boogie told me on the telephone. Tell me about the Resource Council or whatever it's called.'

'We found fifteen hundred breeding pairs and an unknown number of single birds ranging from British Columbia to northern California.'

'We?'

'The Fish and Wildlife Service. But the Resource Council found twenty-two hundred breeding pairs and said the population has been increasing by one percent a year since 1986. They concluded that spotted owls do just fine in second-growth trees from thirty to sixty years old. My aching butt!'

'Is that complete fiction? Wouldn't it be hard to fake something like that?'

'They did most of their work in redwoods in northern California. The spotted owls living farther north in Oregon and Washington are far more reliant on old-growth timber. If you cut the Douglas fir on the Olympic Peninsula, the owls there are history.'

'But what about the differences in numbers? They're claiming fifty percent more breeding pairs than you.'

Jenny turned up the palms of her hands and shrugged. 'To be honest, it beats me where they found all those owls.'

'And you must be what, an ornithologist?'

Any second she'd hit me with it, I knew: Well, Larry or Robert or David says blah blah and et cetera, to which I would be required out of courtesy to ask, stupidly, Larry or Robert or David who?

This was so she could tell me about her chess-champion-philosophy-professor-ex-New York Met boyfriend who had climbed K-2 without oxygen, hiked across the Kalahari Desert, wind-surfed with teenaged athletes off in the gorge, and could get it up four times on a lazy Sunday afternoon.

'Yes, I am,' she said. 'A bird woman for the U.S. Fish and Wildlife Service. If we had our druthers, we'd list the owl as threatened, but the Forest Service wants to sell timber rights to the land to help reduce the deficit.'

'It's Ellin's lawsuit that's got you on the pike now, I take it.'

Jenny nodded. 'He owns the logging rights to several tracts of old-growth Douglas fir in Gifford Pinchot. Unless Gifford Pinchot has a thriving spotted owl population, there'll be no cutting for the Boz, so he claimed our owl count was low, and then the Resource Council hired their own ornithologists.'

'And they found more owls than you did.'

'My boss and I were listed right up there at the top of Ellin's lawsuit, because we were in charge of the Fish and Wildlife Service count that had been accepted by the courts and Congress.'

'So now what happens?' I said.

'So now we go back to the disputed Gifford Pinchot tracts and count owls again. We don't have a hint as to where Ellin's people found all those owls. But if they signed affidavits saying they found owls, we have to assume they found owls.'

I said, 'Your boss received a bunch of threatening letters from pissed-off loggers, as I recall.'

'We received a lot of hate mail, and you're right, most of it was addressed to

Lois Angleton. My boss. But they were aimed at me also. Several of them referred to 'those women,' meaning Lois and me.'

I said, 'These are heavy stakes to be decided by a study headed by just two people. I don't think that helps any.'

I could see the lights of Hood River coming up. 'The Dalles is another twenty miles down the road. You want to pull in here or keep on trucking?'

'The Dalles is fine,' she said. 'You going to Sixkiller on this job?'

'Oh yes, my clients live about halfway between Sixkiller and Calamity.'

'Ahh, maybe we'll be seeing each other there.'

3

The Case of the Murdered Owl

We rode in silence for a few minutes; then Jenny said, 'You're a detective, Mr. Denson. I bet you like puzzles. Let me tell you about a spotted owl we found flattened outside of Sixkiller. Murdered, actually. A real mystery for you. I'd like to know what you think.'

'Go for it,' I said.

'When an animal gets run over on the highway, it's the state's job to clean the mess up, and if the animal's on the list of threatened species, they try to give us a call.'

I said, 'I think I read about this in the papers. Do you ordinarily find owls flattened on the highway? I thought they were forest feeders.'

'You probably did read about it. It had its few days of fame. And no, we don't ordinarily find them on the highway;

you're right on the money, Mr. Detective. First, this was at the edge of Gifford Pinchot, which is the source of all this legal wrangling, and second, we wondered how on earth a spotted had come to be flattened on a highway — that almost never happens with an owl, much less a spotted. We wanted to find out what it had been eating that would bring it down out of the forest and onto the highway.'

'Our Fish and Wildlife Service in action. Just dig into that yummy owl shit. Boy, oh, boy.'

Jenny grinned. 'It's not quite that bad. Raptors swallow their prey whole. They regurgitate the feathers, fur, and bones in the form of a dry ball of fur and bone. They do this a couple of times a day — once before they go out hunting at night, and usually once in their nests, where these balls of fur and crunched bones pile up.'

'A professional hunter of fur-ball puke. Pretty esoteric stuff.'

'These balls can tell us what the owl has been eating the previous twelve hours.

Everything is packed in there. All we have to do is pick it apart and take a close look under a microscope.'

'And what do they eat?'

'Small mammals about ninety percent of the time — squirrels and wood rats and deer mice mostly. They can take a jay or nuthatch or grosbeak or bat on the fly. They'll take a moth, too, and if crickets get too annoying they'll scarf up a few of them. But they don't scavenge on the highway. Do you know how to wring a chicken's neck?'

I had grown up on a farm. Of course I did. I grabbed an imaginary chicken neck with my right hand and whipped it round and round in a short, hard snap.

'A blow from a tire doesn't twist a bird's neck like a corkscrew. Lois and I saw right off that this owl wasn't killed by an automobile or truck. Owing to the owl's unusual anatomy, it takes a determined effort to wring one's neck. An owl's eyes are both on the front of its face like humans', and like us it has binocular vision — which gives it good depth perception. If you have an eye on either side of a beak or snout, you can effectively see two ways at once; we humans have to turn our necks or shoulders to look from side to side. An owl can turn its neck one hundred and eighty degrees, which means it can face you and swivel its neck directly to its rear.'

'You're saying a neck like that has some give to begin with.'

'It sure does. Somebody wanted to make sure that owl was dead. As far as we're concerned it was murder, nothing less.'

'Did it have a fur ball in its stomach? What was in the fur ball?'

Jenny bit her lower lip. 'We didn't get to find out. When we got back to Portland, we found we had picked up the wrong carcass. The workers had collected two flattened owls, one great horned and one spotted, and we were laughing and having a good time, and we apparently grabbed one and pitched the other in the man's garbage can. I don't know how we did it. It truly was an accident, a screw-up. What more can I say?'

'What happened to the great horned owl?'

'Somebody had nearly eliminated its torso with a shotgun. It was worthless for examination. We called the maintenance workers right back, but it was too late; the spotted was gone. Lois was distraught about what happened and made the mistake of telling a reporter about it, and she used the word murder. Of course, the newspaper and television people just loved the story about the spotted owl that had been murdered near Sixkiller, and shortly afterwards, we even got a letter from some nut saying he was going to twist our necks just like that owl's.'

'What happened then?'

'The police took the note for analysis and asked our cooperation to keep the threat out of the papers, and so far it has been.'

'Did the letter writer admit to killing the owl — '

'Murdering.'

'Murdering the owl, or was he just going to copy the killer's MO using your necks?'

'He didn't say either way, but if we'd been FBI agents, you can believe the woods would be swarming with G-men. The same if we'd been Washington State patrolmen. But owl counters from the Fish and Wildlife Service?' She said nothing for a few moments, looking out at the blackness.

As we came around a curve to the right, the lights of The Dalles Dam shone up ahead. In a few minutes I'd have to give her up and head back up the river.

Jenny said, 'That owl was murdered. Spotted owls are just about the friendliest of all owls and make wonderful pets. Who would want to murder one?'

'Some asshole. When does your recount begin?'

'Sunday night. With Bosley Ellin's people trailing after us and staring over our shoulders — that and screwballs sending us threatening letters. We'll work Sunday night through Thursday and take Friday and Saturday off.'

'Are you ready, do you think?'

'Our count was accurate the first time, and it'll be accurate now. If there are spotted owls out there, we'll find 'em.'

'Atta girl.'

4

Antidote for Existential Angst

We drove in silence for a few minutes; finally, I said, 'By the way, there are a couple of motels and gas stations just around the next bend. You can take your pick from the motels — everything from sleaze to businessman sterile. What do you say I buy you a cup of coffee before I head back?'

'Sure, a cup of coffee sounds good,' she said.

I slowed my bus for the off ramp. 'I can see why you'd get a little jumpy. A guy crazy enough to wring an owl's neck for the hell of it . . . '

'It's spooky,' she said.

'If I were you I'd sleep with one eye open in the manner of John Wayne in Apache country.'

On that cheery note, I pulled up in front of the Cascade Café, which, according to the hoo-hoo painted on the window, had a special on chicken-fried steaks. On Sunday you could get all the chili you could eat for a buck fifty.

Jenny MacIvar and I went into the Cascade Café and settled down all cozy in a padded booth with the cold wind outside and hot cups of coffee in front of us, and the hormonal energy began rocking and rolling across the table. We started groping one another with our eyes, wonderful primal foreplay.

Women like this just do not come tooling into my life unattached. They do not. It doesn't happen, but I didn't want to mess up the fun of thinking it might. The lady obviously loved her owls and liked talking about them, and I liked listening. Figured maybe I could pick up some tidbits that would interest Willie.

I liked just about everything about her. Such charming dimples. It was equally obvious that she liked me. We were adults. Big people. We were both tired, and it was late at night.

I glanced at my watch and said, 'What do you think, owl woman, shall we find ourselves a habitat for the night?' My stomach twisted. Was the craven and uncivilized John Denson to be unmasked and sent on his way upriver to seek warmth and succor elsewhere?

But she didn't say hell no. She did not.

She grinned instead and said, 'I say we get ourselves a place with a good view of the river. There've got to be plenty of vacancies this time of year.'

The perfectly grand Jenny MacIvar was right. It may have been a cold and windy night in October on the Columbia River gorge, but there were plenty of vacancies in The Dalles, Oregon, for two simpatico travelers to be thrown in together and push back the existential angst.

We got ourselves a room in the Willicum Motel overlooking the Columbia River. It was a class place: management accepted just about every kind of plastic imaginable, offered both free HBO and Showtime, plus a coffee maker and instant coffee in neat little plastic bags.

The Willicum may have been dumbly named, but the architect was thinking, I'll give him that; he had sprung the couple of extra bucks it took to include skylights so weary travelers, seeking shelter from the travails of the interstate highway, could watch television with awesome Mount Hood looming above them.

Jenny and I rearranged the furniture, winding up with the bed beside the picture window and under the skylight. This gave us a triple wow — gorge, moon, and Mount Hood — without rolling over.

The wind was still howling, but it was a clear night with a startling white moon and stars without end, which lit Mount Hood in spooky relief. The timber on the mountain's flank was a great, gloomy void, and above that rose somber purplish stretches of alpine rock, and still farther — nearly crowned by the moon — stood the profile of the snow-capped peak.

Sweet Jenny's auburn hair spread as a mane upon the pillow, spilling across the cool white sheet. She was long and lean; her legs went on forever and her eyes were green. She thirsted for passion, longed for it, threw herself into the moment.

A svelte filly she was, excited, anxious

for action, jumpy and responsive at the same time. She was loveliest when she was tightest, torso twisted to reveal exquisitely delicate ribs, breathing gone beyond a gallop and her willow of a spine straining, arched against the splendid tension, her skin a sexy sheen of honest sweat.

Later, as we sat cross-legged on the bed, plumb tuckered, sweat drying, bullshitting and sharing a bottle of screw-top red that I had had stashed in my bus, Jenny asked me about Willie. 'Is your Indian partner going to help you with your case at Sixkiller?'

'It's mine unless it's too complicated or I need help with a surveillance. I'm not sure where Willie's off to. He's got some relatives who live just off Deadman Pass on the Umatilla Reservation, but he could be headed for Spokane possibly, or even Portland. Most of the Indians in the Northwest believe Willie's a shaman.'

Her eyes widened. 'He is? Really? A shaman?'

'That's what they say. Take a drive over to Warm Springs sometime or the Yakima

Reservation and ask them about Willie Prettybird. Not bad for a private eye to have someone to check in on the spirit world from time to time.'

'Does he talk to the animal people and all that?'

'Willie's an intuitive. Other people say he's a shaman, not Willie. He has a remarkable sense of anticipation which he says is because he talks to the animal people. If he says a particular hunch was passed on by Elk or Crow or Coyote, who am I to complain?'

'He's always right, then? Dead on the money?'

I laughed. 'Oh, hell no. He screws up too.'

'But better than average.'

'I wouldn't even say that. The two of us are probably about equal, for whatever that matters. There's a rub you have to understand. This particular talent of his can sometimes backfire.'

'A rub?'

'The way Willie explains it is that these spirits could set him straight a hundred percent of the time if they wanted to, but they just don't feel like it. Every once in a while they amuse themselves by playing a little trick on him.'

'A trick?'

'They'll feed him bullshit or throw him a red herring. He says he does his best to stay on their good side, but that doesn't always work.'

'Amazing!'

'That's what I say.'

5

All About Adonis

The next morning over breakfast in the Cascade Café, I decided there was something I had to know for sure. To hell with more talk about spotted owls and Willie Prettybird; I had to know if this dimpled night-riding witch was free from encumbrances.

The auburn hair. The face. The green eyes. The intelligence. The passion. The sense of humor. I ground my teeth, took a deep breath and exhaled, and led with my brains, if not my heart.

'Now you gotta tell me about your old man, Jenny. There has to be one.'

Jenny MacIvar looked as though she'd suddenly remembered she'd forgotten to buy mayonnaise at the grocery store or maybe locked herself out of her car. 'What's that?'

I said, 'You might as well tell me about

your husband or boyfriend and get it over with.'

She blinked. 'My old man?'

'Ronald, or Douglas, or whatever his name is.'

'Oh. Him. His name is Adonis!'

I thought she was joking. Adonis. But no, I could tell by her face she meant it. 'Adonis?' I said stupidly.

'Adonis. It's the truth. His mother was a classics major in college, and when he was born, she insisted he be called Adonis. He was adorable, she says, just adorable. If his father had had his way, he would have been Ralph. Which would you take, Ralph or Adonis? Think about it.'

She had a point, I guess.

'Adonis and I have been living together fourteen months now.'

'That's wonderful,' I lied. 'Fourteen months!' Big strong Adonis. Shit. I hated everything about the bastard without ever having met him. I also wondered why she had it down to the month. Why not 'more than a year' or something?

'I *love* him,' she said — gushed is probably more accurate — aware that the news of Adonis had a cooling effect on my high spirits. It was difficult to tell whether she was trying to convince herself or me with her passionate declaration.

'Oh, well, sure.' I don't know what the hell else I could have said. I mimicked her inside my head: I *love* him. So big deal, lady. Go ahead and love him, but leave me alone.

I must have sat there in the booth of the Cascade Café looking like the most disappointed stupe on the planet, because the beautiful, intelligent Jenny saw fit to explain to me — in what I thought was nothing short of excessive detail — her great love for Adonis.

Of course I couldn't blame anybody but myself. I was the one who had brought up the subject. It was me who had pushed for the jolly full load. I just had to know, couldn't let it go.

'I love him,' she said. 'I truly do.'

She loved him. Okay, so I believed her. But did I want to hear it? Shit, oh dear. I hated the words as they came from her mouth.

Through what had to be the longest cup of coffee in my life, she told me — although only the gods could hazard a guess why I would care — about how Adonis was from a poor family and had worked his way up the hard way, doing every kind of odious and backbreaking job imaginable, and was now politically left-wing and passionately nonmaterialist. He loved the West and lived frugally and was politically sensitive to the have-nots of the world, et cetera. He hiked. He fished. Blah blah blah.

She said Adonis was a superb wildlife photographer who saved every last dime but still had to fly back to Chicago and the East often to beg money from various foundations so he could document the lives of everything from whales and seagulls to baboons and butterflies. She said the bum part was these frequent money-raising trips, but Adonis had to take them; shooting documentaries was an expensive proposition, even though he was careful and costed out every item of a project. He was currently shooting a documentary on owls, which meant he could go with Jenny on her census-taking duties.

Adonis was thoughtful and generous as well as talented. Dogs and kids and old ladies and cripples and ugly people all just loved him. Couldn't get enough of him. Adonis! Adonis! Adonis! He did the dishes. He vacuumed. He left the toilet seat down at night.

I tried not to hear what she was saying, because I wasn't especially fond of dogs pissing everywhere and jabbing me in the crotch with their noses, and he had me on the toilet seat part for sure.

I thought, Come on, lady, don't do this to me. So I took a little detour to get you in out of the cold; it was the civilized thing to do. We wound up having a good time. You don't owe me all this explanation. Life goes on.

Other than Adonis's fund-raising trips, his only fault, as far as Jenny would admit, was that he turned the heat too high when he fried eggs. He had a thing about high heat and eggs and got crabby as hell if she said anything. He just cooked the crap out of eggs.

38

She loved him. I got the picture. I could have told her eggs gave me gas, but I didn't.

We drank coffee in silence for a couple of minutes, and then she called the wonderful Adonis from a pay phone. When she got back, she said Adonis would drive up from their house in Portland and fix whatever was wrong with her car. On top of everything else, it turned out that Adonis was handy with machines and tools; he'd diagnosed the problem on the telephone and was going to fix it himself.

I drove her back to the motel, where she gave me a quick hug and got out. 'Thank you for the good night and the fun, John Denson. I liked telling you about the owls and everything. You're a detective yourself, and you didn't laugh when I said I was going to find whoever it was who murdered that owl.'

God, did she ever smell good. 'You truly are a beautiful woman, and smart, too. I envy Adonis,' I said.

'Thank you,' she said, 'I like you too.'

She meant it, which I suppose accounted

for the catalog of St. Adonis's numerous merits. 'Well, thank you, beautiful Jenny. Good luck with your spotted owls and adios. If perfect Adonis ever takes a powder, you've got my card.'

'Ask your friend Willie to talk to Owl and Mouse for me.'

'I'll do it,' I said.

I waved good-bye and headed down-river on the interstate, this time bucking a head wind, side door still popping. There was no way in hell I could compete with a man whose only real fault was burning eggs. Someone ought to sculpt a wax Adonis and display him in some sort of Domestic Hall of Fame.

For a while back there — before she remembered her loyalty to Adonis — Jenny had really been something. I vowed that next time, by God, I'd keep on driving; to hell with ladies in distress, leave 'em in the cold.

A splendid, blinding orange sun rising at my back, I wheeled toward Portland, where I would cross the Columbia River on the interstate and head north past Vancouver for the turnoff to Sixkiller.

Still, Jenny MacIvar would be at Sixkiller too. Maybe I would yet get a chance to make her forget Adonis the incomparable, photographer of the birds and bees, destroyer of fried eggs.

She loved him, she had said most passionately. That she had once loved him was obvious. But now? I didn't believe a word of it.

6

The Pleasures of Calamity

I had to push the squared-off snout of the VW microbus against a wind the guy at the gas station said was gusting to sixty miles an hour — according to the weather dude on the radio.

When I was a kid, the westward tilt of the trees and shrubs in the gorge didn't mean a whole lot more than that the wind never stopped. It was more of a pain in the ass than anything else. Later, the wind was a source of tourist bucks in Hood River on the Oregon side and White Salmon on the Washington shore; wind-surfers from all over the world gathered for races. The surfers loved the ever-blowing crisp wind, and there must have been close to a hundred of them just whipping over the water, holding on to their colorful sails, backs arched, arms outstretched.

I sat forward in my seat and held on to the steering wheel with both forearms for the hour-long white-knuckler to Portland from The Dalles.

Boogie Dewlapp's normal procedure in a case like this was to send a neophyte lawyer from Seattle down to spring the clients from the hoosegow and plead for time to prepare a case. This had been done.

Next, Boogie would hire me, or someone like me, to run a preliminary investigation which he would then study to determine what kind of defense was needed and which of his lawyers was required. He had good ones and bad, beginners and pros, including his brother Olden down in Portland and Boogie himself. If it was an obvious, simple win, he'd assign a beginner. If it was a real twister, or promised headlines or extraordinary fees, the mighty Boog himself might condescend to enter the fray.

Boogie's secretary had reserved a cabin, one of the Kokanee Vacation Cottages, a half mile up the Lewis River from the village of Calamity, Washington

— about sixty miles north of Portland and sixteen miles south of Sixkiller. This was at the southern foot of Goat Mountain, itself due west of Mount St. Helens.

She said the decision to lodge me in Calamity rather than the larger Sixkiller was because Calamity was closer to the Harkenrider residence. Unstated: The Kokanee Cottages were cheaper than anything she could find in Sixkiller.

Boogie had temporarily assigned a lawyer named Wesley Spooner to the case. Boogie said Spooner was a good one, having recently graduated twenty-sixth in his law class at the University of Puget Sound. After springing the Harkenriders, young Spooner was to bring the couple to my cottage tomorrow afternoon so I could hear their version of what had happened.

Willie Prettybird and I had been throwing at a dart tournament in St. Helens, Oregon, when the mountain across the Columbia River popped her cork and lost fifteen hundred feet from her top in one gaudily dramatic Sunday afternoon — in the end trailing a path of ashes across Washington, Idaho, and Montana; it had been quite a show.

While we'd waited our turn at the board, Willie and I had sat on the front steps of the Klondike Tavern and watched the action across the river. Talk about SuperPanavision wrap-around sound or whatever. We were at the right place at the right time; it was as though we were watching the riffling of ten thousand cosmic postcards.

As the smoke and ashes billowed to the heavens on that warm, clear day, Willie went into one of the special trances he entered from time to time. Later, when we were driving back to his friend's place in Portland where we had crashed the previous day, Willie sank into a despondent gloom.

I asked him if he had been talking to the animal people about what had happened on Mount St. Helens.

He said yes, he had. He said the eruption was the result of geologic indigestion, and there had been much roiling and boiling and gurgling in the earth's innards long before the mountain blew its top. He said the long crack in the earth's crust that runs from Alaska to Chile was in fact the earth's ass. The San Andreas Fault in California was this ass opened as wide as possible.

When large amounts of gas built up in the earth's innards, it had to go somewhere. He said we humans had to blow it off if we ate beans or too many onions or eggs. He said the earth's gas could blow almost anywhere along this enormous ass. Willie said the geologists from the University of Washington could call it 'cone building' if they wanted, but the truth was that the lava that came oozing out was plain old shit.

The process of building mountains was simple: Mount Rainier and Mount St. Helens and Mount Hood were all great mounds of manure that had collected around the geologic orifices along the great ass-crack.

Willie said most of the animals felt the geologic gurgling, which human scientists measured as vibrations. They sensed the danger at hand, and there was a silent, spooky calm among the animal people on Mount St. Helens. Then they ran and flew and swam for their lives. Some made it, but most didn't.

He said the birds and most of the deer and coyotes at the base of the mountain made it out, but smaller animals and almost all those living at higher elevations on the flanks of the mountain had perished. The animal people were in mourning, he said.

'This was a sort of geological fart, then,' I said.

'It happens to the best of us, Chief,' he said. 'Part of life. That was a real cheek flapper today. Here, take this one.' Willie leaned on one cheek, threatening to let me have it with a blast, but it was a bluff; his innards were empty.

I asked him which one of the animal people told him the fate of the animal people on Mount St. Helens, and he said it was Owl. Owl had told him.

★ ★ ★

I had a sandwich in Produce Row in Portland and headed north on I-5 in the early afternoon. It began to rain lightly as I turned off the freeway and sped along the narrow highway toward Calamity. There was a hotly fought contest being waged for sheriff of Skamania County, and both sides apparently had handsome budgets for roadside signs, because they were everywhere.

The incumbent, Bert T. Starkey, had commandeered a cool-and-responsible blue for his signs, leaving the challenger with a pay-attention-to-me-and-throw-that-asshole-out red. Starkey had apparently spent a bundle on billboards. It seemed like there was a BERT T. STARKEY FOR SHERIFF billboard around every curve, and they were all the same: the portly, genial-looking Starkey, hawking his 'experience, honesty, and integrity.'

Sheriff Starkey was obviously a savvy politician; he wasn't about to squander his billboard money on something cute but unproductive, and he did not make the mistake of overestimating the intelligence of the voters of Skamania County. With such a witty and memorable slogan as 'experience, honesty, and integrity,' he had to be a cinch for reelection.

I wondered: did experienced and honest old Bert T. himself lead the raid on the Harkenrider place? A fifty-plant pot bust on the eve of the election must have been cause for the popping of champagne corks in the Starkey household. Yes sir, the benign sheriff looking out at pass-ersby from his many billboards had struck a blow against the evil drug barons.

I came at last to Calamity, which was located at a broad bend of the Lewis River where it was intersected by the south-flowing Lucky Buck Creek. Sixkiller was sixteen miles north on the Lucky Buck.

Judging by the tackle-and-bait shop next to the Texaco station and Mini-Mart, the RV park at Calamity — all hookups for six bucks a night — was a favorite for salmon and steelhead fisher-men working the Lewis and the Lucky Buck and their feeders.

In cosmopolitan downtown Calamity there was no lacking in opportunity to have a hot time.

If you wanted a bowl of steaming chili with chopped onions and cheese on top, or a hamburger with an impressive slice of Walla Walla sweet shoved in there, you could go to Delbert's Awful Onion drive-in, which had a ten-foot plastic onion on the roof.

If you had a hankering for a draft Rainier dry or a glass of blackberry wine, or wanted to listen to a country and western band on a Friday or Saturday night, you could go to the Hog Wild Saloon.

On your way home, if you wanted, you could continue a cheap bender with a quick stop at the Mini-Mart for a couple of quarts of Rainier's Ale, known locally as the Green Death, owing both to its potency and to the color of its bottle.

If you wanted a breakfast with everything virtually steeped in butter, a real heart-stopper, that is, eggs cooked in butter, potatoes fried in butter, toast slathered with butter — bacon strips allowed to simmer in their own pool of fat — you chose a place like Minnie's Café, which was a cozy little log cabin of a place with smoke drifting happy-happy out of a stone chimney on one side.

Such were the pleasures of Calamity.

Looking back through my rearview mirror at the plastic onion atop Delbert's, I remembered the county fair when I was a kid; the crafty Lions Club or American Legion always saw to it that a pile of onions was kept frying on the grill, the wonderful smell luring customers across the sawdust.

Calamity behind me, I continued upriver on the Lewis — that is, to the east — for a half mile until I arrived at the dilapidated Kokanee Vacation Cottages where I was to plant the flag of Boogie Dewlapp.

The Kokanee was so named because of a fish that looked like a large trout but which was technically a land-locked salmon and which, I assumed, was to be found in a nearby lake or one of the reservoirs on the Lewis.

My stomach began to growl when I checked into unit number nine to stow my gear.

The cottages were artifacts of the early fifties; they had been repainted over the years but probably never remodeled. The single small room in number nine contained a diminutive refrigerator with a motor that growled; a two-burner gas stove; a card table with a warped top; four folding chairs; an open closet; a television set; a bureau with cigarette burn marks on the top; a dilapidated double bed with a suspect mattress, and a complicated metal contraption in one corner that was actually a fold-out bed. A beige throw rug had been flopped over the linoleum floor, and there was a small bathroom with a toilet and metal shower. The air smelled of mildew and pine oil. The floor sagged dangerously in the middle.

And it was cold, oh, so cold. I turned the thermostat up to sixty-eight degrees, wondering if it was still connected to the old-fashioned baseboard electrical heater. The top drawer of the bureau contained an extra blanket, which I flopped on the bed.

In my experience, a hot shower was essential after an exhausting day on the road, and I peeled 'em off to go for it. Unfortunately, this shower, a metal-walled cubicle, was crudded up with what I took to be mold, but which could have been killer ooze from a science fiction movie. Owing to mineral buildup, the shower head was only about one-fourth functional, but the water was hot, and by gyrating nimbly to catch the few errant squirts that made it through the crud, I managed to get wet.

Feeling invigorated, if not exactly cheerio, I stepped out, checking my feet for clinging yuck. I dried off on a threadbare towel, and as I was sitting on my bed lacing my shoes, an inch-and-a-half-long cockroach started cruising across the floor like a happy dinosaur; I lunged at him and speared the son of a bitch with my shoe. Dumb Fu John Denson. No bug fucks with him.

My stomach growled. I was hungry. I cranked up my bus and headed for Calamity, deciding I'd check out Delbert's Awful Onion and come back and hit the sack early.

7

He Meets the Wonderful One

At Delbert's Awful Onion you had your druthers; you could order your food through a little window or go inside and sit at a booth. There were those who declined for aesthetic reasons to eat in one of these theaters of the mundane, preferring to dine in their cars with coffee dripping on their stomach and Thousand Island dressing on their crotch.

I was neither timid nor a snob; no, sir, I was an adventurer! I strode manfully inside and stood, thick-witted, humbled by Delbert's vast menu on the wall. I resolved not to be intimidated.

How sweet life must be to have so many options, but I couldn't decide. I could have had a chicken burger if I had wanted, or a taco burger or bacon burger or barbecue burger or mushroom burger or whatever-the-hell-I-could-possibly-want kind of burger, but apparently only an out-and-out prole ever ordered an ordinary hamburger or cheeseburger.

I listened to the sizzle and pop of boiling fat as I considered the least harmful and best-tasting options among the artery-clogging choices. Perhaps it was the case that ordinary hamburgers and such items as chocolate malts were rarely ordered, archaic offerings, pleasing to old people and kept on the menu to keep the Awful Onion in touch with its colorful roots and traditions. I wasn't without my pride; I didn't want to peg myself as a prole.

Would I have the nerve to embarrass myself by ordering a cheeseburger? Did I have the hair?

The waitress was a short, plump teenager with breasts that squashed up against the counter in the manner of safety cushions proposed for new cars — in a crash, one smashed into an embracing pillow rather than glass and metal.

I broke the suspense. 'I would like one of your odious but splendid chiliburgers, please, loaded with all the awful onions you can muster and a cup of coffee. Why, I've heard about these awful onions of Delbert's from Washougal to Puyallup and beyond.' I sang a song for her.

'*Delll-bert's awww-ful onnn-ions*
Taste   grrreat   when   friiied   with
   grunnn-ions.'

She looked momentarily puzzled.
'They're little fish they catch at night in the surf in southern California.'
'That's right. I have a cousin in San Diego.' She wrote down my order and gave me a nine of diamonds which she would call when my order was ready.
I turned, wondering if I shouldn't have ordered some onion rings too, and there, sitting in a booth, a good-looking blond of about forty was watching me have my fun from over the shoulder of a tall man with a head as bald as Brynner's dome.
The bald one was reading something,

and his eyes were on the table. I grabbed a pile of newspapers intended for Delbert's customers and headed for an empty booth just behind him.

As I walked past their table, I noted that el baldo was wearing a photographer's vest, the pockets of which bulged impressively with high-tech gizmos and doodads.

I flopped down in the booth and opened the first newspaper, the Vancouver *Columbian*. There, on the front page, was a story on the spotted owl count in the Gifford Pinchot National Forest that was to begin Sunday night. It pointed out that the action would actually start at noon Saturday with a protest parade in Sixkiller by the Committee for Loggers' Solidarity. Jenny MacIvar's nemesis Bosley Ellin was to be grand marshal.

The story was printed beside a photograph of the blond woman sitting behind me. She was Dr. Lois Angleton, the woman in charge of the count and Jenny MacIvar's boss. I wondered if I could hear Lois Angleton's conversation with the bald one. Yes, I could.

Then she mentioned his name. Adonis! The guy was wearing a photographer's vest. Adonis, the sainted one. His last name was Northlake. Had to be.

They were talking about feminism. Angleton was saying she was glad Northlake was a feminist. She couldn't stand being around men who weren't feminists.

Northlake grunted. From both the tone and enthusiasm of his grunt, he made it clear that he agreed with Angleton.

Now if Northlake had said he agreed with most rational feminists and supported their just complaints — which were legion, heaven knows — that would have been one thing. Even I did that. But I wondered what kind of approval rating Northlake had to achieve in order to qualify as a flat-out, no-arguments-asked feminist. A one-hundred-percent kowtow? And by what woman's standard? Betty Friedan's? Barbara Stanwyck's?

I knew if I got to know Northlake, I might like him. He was probably a hell of a guy, just like Jenny said. In my opinion, however, he was an asshole of assholes for the sole reason that he had gotten to Jenny MacIvar before me; I was in no mood to give him a break or be generous in any way. I wanted to rise up goddammit and shout over the back of the booth: One does not deliver one's balls to an ideological chopping block to earn a woman's respect, fuckhead! One does one's best to behave in a civilized manner, and let one's actions do the talking!

'Nine of diamonds,' the waitress called.

That was me. Food. I walked to the counter to retrieve my plastic basket of grub and cup of coffee. Lois Angleton watched me as I headed back; I slowed and said, 'Excuse me, ma'am, but I believe I may have seen your photograph in the Vancouver *Columbian*. Are you by any chance the ornithologist in charge of the owl count?'

'Yes, I am.'

I put my chiliburger and coffee down on my table. I said, 'Dr. Lois Angleton, is that the name?'

She was pleased that I'd remembered her name. 'Yes, it is. And this is Adonis

Northlake, the nature photographer.'

I shook Northlake's hand. 'I picked up Jenny on the freeway last night when her Volvo broke down. I suppose she mentioned it.' Well . . . just a little of it.

'Mr. Denson, the detective. Yes, she did, when I fetched the Volvo this morning. She was very grateful, by the way. She said you turned around to go back and get her out of that wind. I want you to know I appreciate it too.'

I resisted the urge to run my fingers through my hair, an unmanageable thatch in which each hair took its own determined, eccentric path to the heavens. This bordered on Einstein and movie madmen hair; Chief Dumbshit hair, Willie Prettybird called it. I wanted to bend over and shake my unruly thatch in Northlake's face: See here, Light Bulb, this is real hair; go ahead, rub oils and elixirs on that glassy dome of yours, see where it'll get you.

I wondered just how much Northlake knew about my encounter with Jenny, but decided under the circumstances the less said the better. If she was going to be here for the owl count, I'd bump into her one way or the other. 'My friend Willie is something of an expert on animal calls — or so he says. He's tried to teach me a few of the easier ones, but I don't think I'm worth a damn. You're an expert on owls, Dr. Angleton. I'd like to hear what you think.'

Lois Angleton liked to be doctored. 'Sure, let me hear your stuff.'

'I'm not very good at this, but I'll give it a go.' I couldn't picture the woman killing anyone, but Northlake was another matter. I cupped my hands. I couldn't remember what a spotted owl was supposed to sound like, but there was one I did remember: '*Hoo . . . hoo-hoo-hoo . . . hoo.*'

'A great horned,' she said.

'I think I got the count right, but the pitch is far too high.'

She said, 'You know they're the most fierce is why you remembered it, I'll bet. A great horned owl can take down a duck or a pheasant or a grouse if it wants, did you know that? It can hunt woodchucks and raccoons. It can even take down a red-tailed hawk if it wants. Incidentally, a spotted owl is no match for a great horned owl, and when the great horned owl invades a spotted owl's habitat . . . '

'Then the spotted owl takes off,' I said. That's what Willie Prettybird had told me.

'They're gone. History,' she said. 'A spotted owl just can't defend itself against a great horned owl. It won't even try.'

Northlake said, 'The great horned owl loves loggers, Mr. Denson. When a timber outfit clear-cuts a stand of trees, they're setting the table for the great horned owl to take the forest next door. Is the man who taught you the calls the Indian friend you told Jenny about?'

'That's him.'

'You have an Indian friend who knows bird calls?' Angleton said.

Northlake said, 'If Jenny got it correct, Mr. Denson has an Indian friend who helps him out part-time with his detective work.'

'Ahh, I see. And he calls birds?'

'He's an ace.' Jenny had obviously told him quite a bit.

'Won't you join us at our booth?' Angleton said.

'Well, thank you.' I retrieved my chiliburger and coffee from the empty booth. 'I see where they're having a protest parade Saturday.'

'Let them protest all they want. We've got the nests mapped, and we're ready to go. Sunday night we get down to the nitty-gritty.'

'A once-and-for-all no-bullshit count this time.'

'Absolutely. Bosley Ellin will have his hired ornithologists watching over our shoulders. They either bitch now or forever hold their peace.'

'Ellin's timber posse,' Northlake said.

'Everybody agrees on the nests, but the spotteds themselves could be gone and other birds using those nests. Nests prove little.'

'So where are you folks holed up?' I said. 'Do you have a spotted owl central command?'

Angleton smiled. 'We've taken over the St. Helens Motel in Sixkiller. It's not the Waldorf-Astoria, but it's good enough for owl counters. And what about yourself, Mr. Denson? As they say, what brings you up to this neck of the woods? I bet they don't get a lot of private investigators in Skamania County.'

'Well, I've got a couple who went off on a three-week vacation and when they got back, Sheriff Bert T. Starkey swooped down upon them and found fifty marijuana plants drying in an abandoned building on their place. Of course, the couple kept a cool head and telephoned Boogie Dewlapp — you may have seen him on television.'

Northlake raised his eyebrows. 'Boogie Dewlapp?' He said this as though he were saying, 'Snot?'

Boogie was a popular object of derision, I knew that. He was to legal advertising in Washington what the crew-cut Tom Peterson was to appliances down in Portland. You got the best deal possible with Boogie or Tom — or so they claimed in their commercials. Peterson offered 'a happy place to buy,' and Dewlapp provided 'expert, affordable legal advice for everyone. First visit free of charge.'

Boogie Dewlapp had paid my rent on

more than one occasion. Under Adonis's casual sneering, a truly dedicated samurai or ninja detective — if he was to properly honor his liege — was supposed to maintain his cool, but it was tough. I can be hip up to a point.

'The young man and his wife say they're innocent,' I said mildly. 'I suppose somebody ought to check their story out. I know I'll do my damnedest.'

'Oh, well, of course,' Northlake said. He didn't want to come off as being illiberal on top of being a kowtowing baldie.

I took a bite of my chiliburger. It was delicious.

'Say, tell me,' I said, 'just how does one go about counting owls in the first place? They're nocturnal, aren't they? Surely they don't line up and count off for you! Just what is it you do?'

8

They Fly in Ghostly Haunts

Lois Angleton liked birds or she wouldn't have become an ornithologist. She was pleased to tell me the right way to count spotted owls. She said, 'Ahh, this is the detective in you, eh, Mr. Denson? You do like puzzles.'

'I like birds, too. For a while I got all involved in carving and painting ducks and shorebirds.' So Jenny had told Northlake about me? How much did she tell him? Just that I had picked her up after her car broke down, or more?

Angleton said, 'You gave up your carving?'

'That's when I had a girlfriend whose father had a band saw and cutting knives. It was fun, but now I float around too much to lug all that gear with me. How do you people find a spotted owl, anyway? Do you walk around hooting in the woods?' I took a sip of coffee, thinking about Jenny.

'It's difficult for a human to imitate a spotted owl call and get a reply, but they'll respond to a tape of a real bird.'

'I was close, then. You walk around in the woods playing taped owl calls.'

Angleton finished her coffee.

The gallant Northlake popped to his feet. 'I'll get us refills. Would you like another cup, Mr. Denson?'

'Sure. Thank you,' I said, and drained the one I had.

'Thank you, Adonis.' Angleton, a thoughtful finger to her chin, watched Northlake stroll coolly to the counter. 'The first thing we try to do is find their nests, Mr. Denson, and see if there's any fresh spotted owl droppings. In New Mexico and California spotteds live in caves or crevices on cliffs, but we're looking for nests high atop broken trees or in hollowed-out trunks. When a spotted is forced out of an area, other birds take over the nest, so we can't rely on simple nest counts.'

'I see. Then you have to find the birds themselves?'

'At night. A lot of owls feed at dawn or dusk, when the game is active, but a spotted feeds solely at night.'

Northlake was back with the coffee. He said, 'Out there with things that go bump in the night, Mr. Denson.'

Angleton said, 'It's hard to pinpoint a call in a pitch black forest, so we usually split into pairs about fifty feet apart and use a crude form of triangulation. When you hear one, you have to pay attention.' She cupped her hands around her eyes and moved her head slowly from side to side. 'Then, when you get a call, you pinpoint the bird with your flashlight.'

'Ahh, their eyes reflect the light.' I found myself listening to Lois Angleton and thinking about Jenny and Northlake at the same time. It was just impossible not to, with Northlake sitting there.

'Yes, they do, but all owls are not all the same. Most of them have yellow eyes, and they'll reflect the flashlight from almost any angle. Spotteds have dark blue eyes that look brown, and what you have to do is make sure you're looking right down the beam of light at the owl or you won't see the reflection. The best way is to put the flashlight right beside your ear.'

'Doesn't the flashlight spook 'em?' Jenny had told him that I had an Indian partner. How much else had she told him? Oh, by the way, Adonis, I jumped in the sack with the guy when we got to The Dalles. And what was the occasion of her telling him about me? A casual, oh-by-the-way sharing, or an all-cards-on-the-table fight?

'The owls appear not to associate the light with danger. At least not at first. They usually give us a few minutes of shining a flashlight in their eyes before they take off.'

'Where do you go to find them? I mean, where is it they hang out?' Jenny hadn't hesitated to jump in the sack with me, yet she hadn't struck me as promiscuous.

'They're called spectral owls in early texts, because they're very timid and people just saw ghostlike flashes of them in the deepest, darkest forests. In fact, we believe they need a crown closure of up to eighty percent in order to survive.'

'Crown closure?' All that going on about how wonderful and perfect Northlake was. Guilt. That's what it was, pure guilt. Jenny had once loved him dearly, but something had changed.

'That's when the limbs of the treetops take up eighty percent of the space — we're talking gloomy, Little-Red-Riding-Hood kind of woods. They're also thirsty little fellows and take frequent baths, so they like a dependable stream nearby. Give them a steep and remote canyon, and they'll take it. In Oregon they ordinarily nest from sixty-five to a hundred and fifty feet high on a Douglas fir that's lost its top to wind or lightning — trees from two hundred to six hundred years old.'

'How much of this kind of territory do they need to survive?'

'We think somewhere between three hundred to six hundred acres for each pair of owls; both sides finally settled on five hundred and sixty acres, but the quarreling hasn't stopped. Six hundred acres is one square mile, remember. The big timber outfits harvest their private stands every sixty to seventy-five years. The government stands hit the ax every seventy-five to eighty years. When the old trees are gone, they're gone, that's it, no more. Nationally, we only have ten percent of the forest we did in the eighteenth century. Ultimately, that systematic destruction of the forest is what the environmentalists are all worked up about.'

Six hundred acres for one pair of owls? I had to get my mind off Jenny MacIvar and on the owls. 'I take it the remaining spotteds mostly live in parks and national forests.'

'That's right. The domain of the Forest Service and the Bureau of Land Management, which periodically auctions off tracts of the timber to lumbermen like Bosley Ellin.'

'The evil bearer of the chain saw.'

'Bastards,' said Northlake.

Angleton tightened her mouth. 'Not only does the spotted owl have to dodge chain saws, it also has to keep an eye out

71

for the great horned owl.'

'What does the great horned owl do?'

'It eats spotted owls.' She paused. 'Among other prey.'

'So, tell me, Dr. Angleton, what does a spotted owl sound like?'

'Well, that depends on what kind of mood it's in. The main spotted owl call has four hoots, or syllables. A short hoot and a pause, two more short hoots, a longer pause, then a longer hoot. The bird books usually transcribe this as *Whoo . . . HoWhoo . . . Whooo*. One of their other calls sounds like the yelping of a dog or coyote except that it comes in four notes always and doesn't rise in pitch. If a spotted owl is spooked or a female thinks her young are in danger, she'll make a *whee-e-e* sound that rises in the middle like a siren.'

I'd long since finished my chiliburger, and I knew everything there was about counting owls. I checked my wristwatch. I rose and said, 'Well, it's getting late. When you're Boogie Dewlapp's main man in Calamity, you've got responsibilities.'

They were ready to go too. We all rose

and said our goodbyes. 'Well, say hello to Jenny for me,' I said to Northlake. I wanted to say more but dared not.

As I sat on the cold plastic seat letting the bus's engine warm, I thought about Jenny MacIvar and the marvelous Adonis Northlake. Jenny had only two bad things to say about him: he turned the heat up too high when he cooked eggs, and he spent too much time yo-yoing back and forth to the East on fund-raising trips.

If Jenny had been joking about the eggs, a fault she could put up with, she was serious about the trips. It was hard to believe all the environmental and bird-lover money was in the East. But maybe it was. In any event, the trips really bothered her.

9

The Cat of Purring Dreams

My mind was on Adonis Northlake's bald head and uppity attitude toward Boogie Dewlapp when I got back to the Kokanee Vacation Cottages. I fumbled momentarily for my keys, then opened the door to my cabin, but when I started to reach for the light, I knew immediately that I had a visitor.

I felt a sudden surge of adrenaline.

Willie Prettybird said, 'If you'd leave it off, I'd appreciate it, Denson.'

He was sitting in a folding chair turned backwards, looking out of the window at the courtyard and parking lot. He was dressed only in his underwear, and I assumed from the gravity of his voice that he was either just entering or coming out of one of his contemplative trances.

I said, 'You about scared the bejesus

74

out of me, you silly bastard. Don't do that.'

'I want to sit and talk. No electricity.'

I left the light off, closed the door, and started unbuttoning my shirt. I stripped down to my shorts and went in to brush my teeth, wondering why it was that Willie had chosen to catch up with me in Calamity.

I took the toothbrush out of my mouth long enough to say, 'Let me make a guess, Willie. You're up here because you like to lose at cribbage.'

Willie said nothing.

'Not cribbage? Well, then how about the spotted owl recount?'

He stirred. My eyes had become adjusted to the pale light, and I could see him more clearly. 'I came here because this is where they're going to start.'

I poured myself a glass of water and rinsed out the toothpaste foam.

'Owl told me a spotted owl was murdered and its body dumped onto the highway near Sixkiller, where it was flattened by log trucks.'

A murdered owl. He agreed with

Jenny's conclusion, but of course the story of the flattened owl had been in all the newspapers. I sat cross-legged on my bed, still confident that there was logic to everything.

A woman was squatting in the center of the pull-out bed. I was momentarily spooked. She sat watching me, her arms around her knees; she'd been there listening to us from the moment I arrived.

She had huge eyes, great black pits in the dim light, and wore cotton runner's warmups, the old-fashioned kind — out of what I called sweatshirt material and with the classic hood.

Was she Willie's girlfriend or sister or cousin or what?

She made no attempt to introduce herself. When she saw that I had spotted her, she glanced at Willie with her extraordinary eyes and put a finger to her lips; she didn't want to put me off, but she wanted me to listen to what Willie had to say. Introductions would come later.

Willie said, 'Spotted owls have a reputation for being friendly to the point of affectionate, Denson. They make wonderful pets. For someone to deliberately wring one's neck is unspeakable. Imagine wringing the neck of a canary for the hell of it. It's like knocking a puppy in the head.'

'And the animal people are pissed, I take it.' I talked to Willie but I watched the woman. 'Owl and the gang.'

Willie laughed bitterly. 'Pissed? Sorely pissed is the word, Chief. They're calling it an execution, and they want justice.'

'I can imagine.'

'Owl said since I work for a private detective part-time, I ought to know something about the investigating business, and I was henceforth to consider myself deputized until the murderer was brought to justice.'

That diverted my attention from the woman in the sweat-suit. 'What in the hell are you talking about, man? Deputized by one of the animal people?' I looked back at the woman.

She gave me a lopsided grin.

'You too, Denson. Both of us.'

I turned. 'Me? Come on now, Willie.'

'That's it, Chief. The animal people met in council and decided the matter.'

The woman on the bed nodded in agreement. Yes, the council had done that. We were deputies of the animal people.

I said, 'If Owl knows all about private eyes and everything, then he ought to know we're supposed to get paid for what we do. I've got work to do up here, Willie, a paying client.'

'You're supposed to be my partner.'

'Oh, shit, Willie.'

'A man's partner! What do you want to do, embarrass yourself? Come on, man.'

The woman on the bed nodded again. Obviously she agreed with him. Did I want to embarrass myself?

I didn't say anything.

'Please don't embarrass yourself, Denson. I don't want to see it.'

The woman shook her head. She didn't want to see that either.

'What is it Owl wants you to do, exactly?'

'Us, Deputy Denson. He wants us to find the truth.'

78

The woman nodded with approval.

'The truth, well, no problem there.'

'Owl says once the truth is known, justice will follow. One of the first things you'll have to do is figure a reason to have a chat with Bosley Ellin.'

'Do you suspect Ellin of murdering the spotted?'

'I think he had something to do with it.'

'Based on what, Willie?'

'A feel.'

'The famous Prettybird intuition. Who's supposed to be my client? Don't tell me Owl, for Christ's sake.' I was going to help Willie out, and we both knew it, but it wasn't fun if I caved in without any resistance.

Finally, in order to please the woman on the bed as much as Willie, I said, 'Okay, I'll come up with a way to talk to Bosley Ellin. It might take me a couple of days to come up with something, and you have to appreciate that I have to take care of my work for Boogie.'

'It's done, then. Thank you, Chief. I appreciate it. By the way, Saturday at noon the Committee for Loggers' Solidarity is holding a protest parade over at Sixkiller.'

'You're going to put me right to work?'

'Bosley Ellin is the grand marshal of the parade. Might as well get on the case.'

The woman on the bed was extraordinarily small, certainly five feet or under, and I would bet not more than eighty or ninety pounds.

Willie had described her to me often enough. This was Donna Cowapoo. Had to be.

Finally, I'd had enough. 'Damn it, Willie, knock off your jabbering for a minute and introduce me to the pretty girl.' I walked across the sagging floor and shook her hand. She had dark hair done up in two pigtails that fell to the small of her back. 'I'm laying ten to one your name is Donna Cowapoo.'

Willie looked around and blinked. 'Oh, hell, yes, I forgot. Donna Cowapoo, this worthless piece of shit is John Denson.'

She said, 'Thank you for helping us out, John.'

'I'll do my best.'

Willie said, 'Let's face it: When you're down to John Denson, you're down to the bottom of the private-eye barrel.'

Donna ignored him. 'You knew my name?' She looked somehow surprised and pleased at the same time. 'How did you know?'

'Willie has been pushing your case for months, if not years. 'Denson, Denson, Denson, you have to listen,' he says. Donna Cowapoo this; Donna Cowapoo that. Hey, let's face it, he lobbied so hard I began to get a little suspicious, if you know what I mean.'

'Willie!' She gave Prettybird a look.

'I thought maybe you were damaged goods of some kind. How was I supposed to know?'

Willie said, 'Aw, for Christ's sake, Denson. He's making this all up, Donna.'

I said, 'Had to be something wrong, is the way I figured it.' I tried to imagine what she looked like with those pigtails of hers combed out and spread over her breasts and down over her naked body.

I thought it must be perfectly grand to

be the man so honored to lie back and use Donna's wonderful butt for a pillow.

★　★　★

Willie didn't mind that I thought these trips of his were hallucinogenic, these trances likely self-induced. He regarded this conclusion as evidence of a limit to my imagination, but by no means fatal to my character. I had to have a physical cause or reason for everything; he understood that. Again and again, I told him, all chance has a cause. Magic is entertaining, but I believe in explanations. Give me logic.

What was important to Willie was that I understood: however illogical his travels and communications with the animal people might seem to me, they were real to him. The predicaments he sometimes got into were equally real to him.

The world of the animal people had its joys and terrors, but it was not a place without understandable rules of conduct. Its sense of history was circular, according to Willie. For example, he said, if a man shits in the middle of the trail and keeps on walking with his eye on the sun, he will one day step square in the middle of his own waste.

Little by little over the six years I had known Willie, I had come to understand this alternate world as he described it. Its inhabitants, although predictable in some ways, were quirky in others. These were not Jesus-type perfect dieties by any stretch of the imagination. They were gods who both screwed up and had a good time. Some Willie liked and could trust; others, he flat-out avoided.

Even if the world of the animal people was a place Willie dreamed up, I was always curious about how it worked; I had no doubt that he possessed a special turn of the imagination, and I was pleased to be privy to his adventures. Whether they were imaginary or not was beside the point.

I remembered him saying once, 'All I ask, Chief, is that you allow yourself to imagine. That won't hurt you, will it? That's all I ask. Accept for a moment and listen. Keep an open mind.'

I did my best, but my mental quirk being what it is, Aristotle was always to be my main man. Cause and effect. A leads to B; B leads to C.

Coyote was Willie's favorite of the animal people, and ordinarily the one he summoned in his trances, although sometimes he would maintain that it was Coyote who had done the summoning. If you're a shaman, you have duties and responsibilities as well as privileges.

Once, when I went with Willie to the village of Taholah on the Quinault Indian Reservation just north of Hoquiam, Washington, I made the mistake of teasing Willie about his frequent disappearing acts.

Later that night when we were all drunker than skunks, a large-bellied man took me to one side and solemnly suggested that I go easy on Willie. He said Willie was Coyote and could only stand being human for short stretches of time.

If that were true, I certainly couldn't disagree with Willie's preferences. Being human did have its drawbacks from time to time.

The large-bellied man said I should be honored to be the white man chosen to be Coyote's earthly companion. In saying this, he seemed genuinely amazed that I could treat Willie so casually.

I envied Willie, if all that hocus-pocus about the animal people and him being Coyote were true. I wouldn't mind having a turn at being a coyote just to see what it was like. I could see Willie and me loping extracool through tall sagebrush, dashing down this or that rabbit trail and snarfing up kangaroo mice as though they were popcorn. In the daytime I'd make furtive dashes toward speeding autos to see if I could frighten drivers into losing control; at night I'd yip and yelp and howl for all I was worth and scare the fertilizer out of all little kids within hearing distance. Just why he — Coyote in Willie form — had chosen to latch on to me was one of life's mysteries.

It was chilly in cottage number nine when the three of us finally got to sleep, I in my bed, Donna in the pull-out, Willie on a fold-out canvas cot I retrieved from the back of my bus; I pulled the covers up around my neck. Outside, I heard a yelping by the lake. Coyotes?

I snuck a quick look at Willie Prettybird to see if he was still there.

He still was. Silly me.

I thought I was in for an uneasy night, but I wasn't. I fell into a deep, restorative sleep.

I dreamed that I was in the woods and heard a great purring. I didn't know where the purring came from, but it enveloped me and was wonderful. Finally, I looked up and on the branch of a spruce tree a sleek panther looked down at me with feline yellow eyes. I looked into the feral depths of those eyes, and the panther purred a soft rumble. The purring enclosed me again, held me. So very soft.

I awoke with a start.

Across the way, Donna Cowapoo was looking at me with those eyes of hers, the dim light making hollows beneath her brow and above her high cheekbones. 'Did you have a dream?' she said.

'I saw a panther sitting on a tree limb.'

'Ahh,' she said.

'It was purring. Humming along like a great, contented pussy cat.'

'It didn't scare you, did it?'

'Gave me a bit of a start was all.'

'A panther! What would you call it, a nightmare or a dream?'

'I'm not sure. I wouldn't call it a nightmare. It wasn't frightening.'

'Ahh, good,' she said and turned over to return to sleep.

It was cold enough to disturb a well-digger's testicles, but I finally fell asleep too. This time there was no purring and no panther.

10

A Penguin Stands Sentinel

When I woke up the next morning, Willie and Donna were gone. Well, they had completed their mission of recruiting me on behalf of the animal people. I had no idea where they were off to, but that was Willie's way, and Willie had a reason for everything, or so he claimed.

I lay there warm and comfy inside my cocoon of blanket; I had to take a leak, but I didn't want to get up. I wanted to lie there in that sublime warmth and maybe dream a little or even go back to sleep. Little pangs in my bladder were slowly and insidiously growing in power.

If I got up and sprinted across the cold floor to the john to get rid of the wee pangs of pain, lying in bed wouldn't be as sweet when I returned. I could warm up my spot in the bed again, sure, but it would never be as sublimely comfortable and cozy. To my knowledge English did not have a word to describe this period of torn emotions, and it was a deficiency.

I lay there, my nagging bladder jabbing me slowly awake, and thought about the day ahead. There was just no way I could investigate the great marijuana fuck-up on the road to Sixkiller without somehow managing to bump into the long-legged Jenny MacIvar. That old scalawag Boogie Dewlapp had inadvertently delivered me into owl country temporarily inhabited by an incomparable woman. Since the Harkenriders were facing jail and were my paying customers, my first day would be devoted to them; the animal people could wait a day.

According to Boogie, Terry and Mary Ellen Harkenrider were at her parents' house in Vancouver, and would stay there until Wesley Spooner brought them to my cottage this afternoon. Meanwhile, I needed to get a feel for the geography along that stretch of the Lucky Buck, to see where it was exactly that they had been busted. The first thing I had to do was take a drive to Sixkiller.

Finally, I had had enough bladder torment, and I leapt out of bed and ran for the toilet, step one on the road to my morning cup of caffeine, which I decided to take at Minnie's Café in Calamity.

I opened the curtains and peered outside. The whole world was a bright, glistening white. A thin layer of frost covered every twig and branch. It was one of those awesomely beautiful but treacherous mornings that take your breath away. Across the parking lot and highway, a mist rose above the Lewis River.

Twenty minutes later, I was outside in the cold using a hot-damn piece of specially cast plastic to scrape the frost off the windshield of my bus; elegant white ribbons of frost curled back onto my hand, and before I was finished my fingers were numb from the cold.

Everything was covered by the delicate frost. The details of the forest receded into the softening mist; glittering white cables held the ends of the Kokanee Vacation Cottages sign; the tops of unpicked beets bent like tiny ghosts in the owners' garden; a wrecked pickup sat white in a field of weeds; elegant, stark-white cattails rose from the edges of the Lewis River.

The heating systems on those old air-cooled Volkswagen engines were notoriously lousy, and mine was no different. Shivering, I waited for several fishermen's rigs to pass before I found a slot in the traffic and set off for Minnie's Café in Calamity. There were fishermen behind me and fishermen in front — in pickups, campers, and vans.

I was wondering what was going on when the traffic slowed, and I could see the beam of a flashlight waggling through the thin fog. A middle-aged woman wearing an orange Day-Glo vest over a puffy nylon coat was going from rig to rig, clipboard in hand. A banner around her shoulder and across her chest said she was with the Sixkiller Jaycees.

She got to me, smiling, her face ruddy from the cold, clipboard at the ready. 'Morning, you joining in the fishing this morning?'

'Fishing? I was wondering.' I glanced at the lineup of fishermen and fishing rigs.

91

'We hold a fishing derby every October here at Calamity. This year it's a three-day event. The proceeds are going to help build a Little League baseball park. Ten-dollar entry fee a day. Five hundred dollars guaranteed to the biggest fish.'

'Well, I think I'll have to pass this time, sorry,' I said. 'These guys have to like their Little League baseball to get out in weather like this.'

She laughed. 'Coffee money this year goes to the Committee for Loggers' Solidarity. Way things are going, they're going to need help.' She motioned over her shoulder with her chin; an amiable-looking man in a safety vest followed close behind her carrying a tray of plastic cups of coffee. His solidarity committee banner said any donation would be appreciated.

'Sure, I'll take a cup. I see by the paper where they're starting their big owl count Sunday.' I dug for my wallet and gave him a buck.

'Thanks.' Breathing clouds of white vapor, he gave me a cup of coffee. 'Somebody'll count their owls for them if they don't watch out.'

'The fishing any good?'

He gave me a sideways grin. He knew I was no fisherman; he'd watched me say no to the entry-fee woman. 'Ain't been worth a damn for almost a week, to tell the truth. Can you imagine paying ten bucks to stand out there in that water?'

'Community spirit,' I said.

'Community something. Your guess is probably as good as mine.'

I drank my dollar cup of loggers' solidarity coffee and inched my bus toward Calamity. On my left, fishermen in rubber waders stood waist-deep in the Lewis River lofting lures gracefully onto the frigid water in front of them. They stood with bodies braced against the current and patiently worked the prospects of the river. They called upon all the experience they could summon to negotiate the hazards and surprises of upwelling and riffle; if they failed, there would be drinking and laughing later on, what the hell, but if they hit it, if they snagged one of those battle-scarred, heart-stopping old lunkers that somebody else always caught, why then you never knew . . .

And this morning — here, witnessed, in a tournament — one of those lunkers might be the three-day winner, might be worth five hundred bucks.

Judging from the number of fishermen on the road and in the water, just about every male in the area wanted an early shot at the five hundred. Never mind that ten bucks was a trifle stiff for a day of suffering. The dough was for a Little League ballpark in Sixkiller; the spirit of the challenge was the thing. I'd been out on the water all day in weather like that; I knew something of what it was like. I knew that later, after a day of suffering cold and wind and eating soggy sandwiches out of a paper bag, the feeling of being totally exhausted was earned and honest and good — a time when an arm around a woman and the enveloping warmth of bed had an elemental meaning that was memorable.

When I got to Calamity, I saw that the Sixkiller Jaycees had erected a large tent in one corner of the RV parking lot where they were selling a 'sportsman's breakfast' of coffee, hotcakes, toast, eggs, fried potatoes, bacon, ham, or sausage, mix 'em and match 'em, all you can eat for seven fifty — proceeds to the Sixkiller Little League diamond.

Despite these goings-on across the street, there wasn't an empty booth left in Minnie's and only one stool left at the counter. I took it. A hearty fire snapped and crackled in the huge fireplace faced with egg-shaped river rocks, and the windows were frosted over. What space wasn't taken up by fireplace or windows was given over to dramatic blowups of Mount St. Helens erupting. One of these pictured Minnie's Café with the eruption in the background.

Sure enough, when you ordered coffee at Minnie's, it was a bottomless cup of mud — the waitress always saw to it that your thick ceramic cup was kept filled with the awful stuff.

Minnie's kept a pile of newspapers for its customers on a small table, and I had grabbed a handful. All of them featured major stories about the pending owl recount and the scheduled protest parade in Sixkiller.

The *Oregonian* reporter had worked the parade into the lead of the paper's front-page story on Jenny MacIvar's owl count. The *Oregonian* was keeping an eye on Sixkiller because there were twelve hundred pairs of spotted owls in Oregon and immense tracts of timber, while there were only five hundred pairs in Washington and fewer trees at stake. The spotted owl may have been a dubious issue, but Oregon's economy was on the line.

The Vancouver *Columbian* ran a boxed notice of the parade on the front page, and had an article on other planned events as well. Bosley Ellin had invited the public to a day-long open house at his mill. At the open house, sawyers would demonstrate their skills with high-speed saws, loggers with double-bitted axes would compete in tree-felling contests, and men in caulked boots would see who could stay atop a spinning, floating log the longest.

The parade down Main Street would begin at noon, and at two P.M., the

Sixkiller High School Desperadoes would take on the Wahtiakum Wolverines in gridiron action.

Dr. Lois Angleton had told the *Columbian* she would not be attending the festivities in Sixkiller; she still had work to do to prepare for the owl count.

She was quoted as saying the original census of owls in Gifford Pinchot was accurate, and she was confident that the recount would give substantially the same numbers. She said she was pleased that there would be 'observers from all sides of the quarrel at this recount, so the number of owls on the tracts in question will be settled once and for all.'

Bosley Ellin, grand marshal of the parade, said there had been 'plenty of owls in Gifford Pinchot all along, but the government scientists just didn't want to count them. It's not that I don't like birds, I do. I used to own a parrot, in fact.'

Dr. Eric Starkey, who had conducted the Audubon Society's count, said, 'The old Boz is full of it up to his ears, as everybody knows.'

I read the newspaper accounts while I packed the fat into my veins, then studied the map of Skamania County that Boogie's secretary had mailed to me. Terry Harkenrider worked in Sixkiller, sixteen miles north of Calamity on the banks of Lucky Buck Creek. A county highway that flanked the south-flowing creek led to Calamity.

Two streams entered the Lucky Buck from the east between Calamity and Sixkiller — the South and North Forks of Jumpoff Joe Creek. The South Fork, along which the Harkenriders lived, was six miles north of Calamity. The North Fork was eight miles away. Jumpoff Joe originated in the mountains of the Gifford Pinchot National Forest, then split to form the two forks.

I finished my breakfast and set off up the Lucky Buck. The winding asphalt highway along Lucky Buck Creek was rumpled and bumpy from years of patchwork maintenance, and the white lay above the water in a wispy blanket.

I geared down to third, then second, creeping along, wary lest an unwary car traveling too fast and too wide on the curve should pop, hello there, from the mist.

Five miles out, I passed a thirty-yard tangle of blackberry bushes and an abandoned Ford pickup with weeds growing through its broken windshield.

The sun was higher and warmer and the fog was clearly thinning. Another mile and I slowed for the bridge across the South Fork of Jumpoff Joe, which was about five or six feet wide. On the far side of the bridge, a paved, two-lane county highway followed the creek up a canyon into the Gifford Pinchot. A sign at the intersection said Sixkiller was ten miles north, which was correct according to my map. The famous Sixkiller Hot Springs was twelve miles east.

I turned up the highway and started watching for the Harkenrider place; the tiny house turned out to be less than a quarter of a mile from the intersection and the land apparently butted up against the Gifford Pinchot.

I idled my bus into the yard and parked it alongside a cement penguin that guarded a brick-edged gravel walkway bisecting a ten-foot-by-ten-foot patch of grass and mud. Lots of tire tracks in the mud. The white clapboard house was roofed with fading red asphalt-composition shingles. The garage next to it was surrounded by engine blocks, axles, and other parts of wounded and dead automobiles, including a rusted Corvair with a missing hood and trunk lid.

I walked around the house, but it was locked and the windows boarded up. I tried the garage door, but it was locked too.

The Harkenriders liked to grow things, that was evident. They had a splendid garden in back of their house. The tomatoes and peppers had pooped out, along with sissy vegetables like cucumbers and eggplants, but they had some good-looking rows of greens still waiting to be harvested, and several kinds of squash.

I walked back out to the narrow highway and, following Boogie's secretary's directions, hiked east, the South

Fork to my right, the Harkenrider property on my left. Twenty yards later, I came to the foundation of another small house that had long ago burned to the ground. Another thirty yards, and I reached the rotting shack where the sheriff had found the drying marijuana plants. Hell, anybody who regularly traveled that highway could see that shack.

The way I figured it, it'd have to be a real sweetheart of a sheriff to bust the Harkenriders on something like that. How the hell were they supposed to know what was stashed in an abandoned shack two hundred yards up the creek? A snarl of blackberry bushes blocked the view from the house. Wesley Spooner ought to get them off on that point alone. Of course, they'd still owe the Boog a bundle for pointing out the obvious to the judge. What a system!

I retreated to my bus and drove back to the Lucky Buck and on toward Sixkiller. The remaining haze thinned and the sun peered through. I sped up, hurrah, and the side door of my bus began its damned rattling again. I shifted down from third to second as I entered the tight curves, a pretend Arturo Nuvolari running the gears of my sleek Ferrari. It was dreamsville as I negotiated the curves: ahead lay an imaginary checkered flag and squealing, eager blonds bearing champagne.

The ridge on my left — across Lucky Buck Creek — was second-growth timber that had been cut some years ago. These trees were large enough to be handsome, maybe ten inches to a foot through, but not the breathtaking cathedrals that old-growth timber could be.

That was reserved for the ridge on my right, which rose to become part of Goat Mountain, about half the size of Mount St. Helens. This grand stand of Douglas fir, stretching to the top of the ridge and beyond, had been spared the logger's ax. It was gorgeous, if your soul wasn't made of tinfoil. Douglas firs were not redwoods — there were redwoods so huge and awesome and inspiring they made a person stop breathing — but they were truly remarkable trees nevertheless.

It was obvious that the Lucky Buck was the line at which the advancing timber industry had somehow been stopped.

At first I thought the preserved forest on the right bank was privately owned because of the tightly strung barbed-wire fences and no-trespassing signs, but according to the road signs, sections of it were part of Gifford Pinchot. The meadows that intervened every now and then on both banks were given over to cud-chewing polled Angus who watched me with indifferent eyes as I went by.

I pulled off to the side of the road and checked my map. The boundary of the national forest, shaded an off-amber on my map, had been set by a bureaucrat with a keen eye and a straight ruler. The presumptuous boundary between private and public ran square and true, whereas Lucky Buck Creek, and the road that followed it, wound back and forth across the surveyor's line. Thus, I assumed, the mapmakers avoided the squiggly border that would have resulted if the creek itself had been used.

About seven miles from Calamity

— halfway between the two branches of Jumpoff Joe — a ridge of second-growth timber had been clear-cut just west of the Lucky Buck. Completely scalped.

One of my clearest childhood memories was of the great, impossible mountains of logs neatly stacked by huge cranes and awaiting the saw, and the cone-shaped burners that stood forty or fifty feet high, from which orange plumes of sparks and cinders rushed at night like fiery ghosts.

I remembered looking out of the back seat of the family car as my father — tailed by a thundering Mack loaded with six-feet-wide logs — negotiated the twists and turns of a mountain road. Nobody talked about old growth or virgin timber then; there were big trees and little trees, and the big trees got cut first.

Over the years, I had noted that the logs on the backs of those big trucks were getting smaller and smaller.

The forest, like life itself, seemed forever to me when I was a child. A ride in western Oregon or Washington meant interminable miles of nothing but trees. So many trees! Who'd have thought that the trees would run out? Certainly few people in those days: logging was pretty much the economy in Oregon and large parts of Washington.

Now, at least, the timber companies used all of the tree for something, and the burners were relics of the past. Every once in a while I saw an abandoned and rusting cone, its days of fiery if wasteful splendor finished, left to the advance of blackberry bushes.

The city limits of the town of Sixkiller, population sixty-three hundred according to the sign at the edge of town, lay on the far side of an old-fashioned metal bridge with visible rivets that had come up a pale green after its last painting.

The Skamania-Pacific lumber mill sat town-side of the Lucky Buck, its entrance the first left on the far side of the bridge. The mill had its own cone, which sat next to a logging museum at the main entrance. Ellin had dammed Sixkiller Creek so as to provide a millpond about a quarter of a mile long.

The mill yards of my youth were piled to overflowing with decks of logs. Here, a five- or six-acre yard that had obviously once stored logs was now next to empty. A single boom of logs covered about thirty percent of the pond, and that was it.

It looked like scores of other small lumber mills I had seen in my travels in the Pacific Northwest and British Columbia. But this was the mill where Terry Harkenrider earned his living driving a Hyster. And this — if the more emotional environmentalists were to be believed — was where the evil Boz stalked.

11

Heartbreak of Swiftly Flowing Waters

My stomach was growling, but I decided to save the details of Sixkiller for parade day; Calamity, although smaller, was closer to the Harkenrider place, increasing the odds of my blundering into useful gossip. For the moment, I had a rough idea of the geography involved and so headed south for Calamity and lunch at Minnie's Café.

Minnie's parking lot was empty except for a plumber's van. The plumber's name was Godlove and the sign on his van said, 'Godlove the plumber, nobody else does.' I parked my bus beside Godlove's van to take a look; a sign on the front door of Minnie's said: CLOSED UNTIL 5 P.M. (OR UNTIL WE GET THE BUSTED PIPE FIXED). Godlove willing, she might have added.

The freezing of Minnie's pipes was not

such a disaster as it might have been, because the Jaycees' beer garden across the road was going full bore. Although the more dogged contestants had sandwiches and coffee without leaving the river, the more laid-back, that is to say, sensible fishermen — who apparently numbered in the hundreds — had assembled inside the tent to drink beer and enjoy what the banner above the tent heralded as:

'Guaranteed the largest and most delicious cheese-burger ever served at a fund-raising event in the Pacific Northwest. Stuff your gut with the Calamity Humongous Burger for five bucks. All the coffee you can drink. Support your Little Leaguers!'

I was left to choose between a Humongous Burger in the Jaycees' big top or Delbert's Awful Onion. I was hungry, although I hadn't spent all morning ass-deep in freezing water.

When in Calamity, eat as the Calamitites, I say; in the spirit of adventure, I walked across the highway and down the

108

paved trail to the RV park where the Jaycees had their tent set up. I smelled frying onions a full twenty yards away, and knew I had made the right decision. Would St. Peter be frying onions at the Pearly Gates? The gates to the cheeseburger big top were manned by two men wearing Jaycees baseball caps. They sat at a card table under a sign that said: IF YOUR GUT ISN'T STUFFED BY OUR HUMONGOUS BURGER, THE SECOND ONE'S ON US. ALL THE FRENCH FRIES YOU CAN EAT AND ALL THE COFFEE YOU CAN DRINK.

That seemed fair enough. I swapped five bucks for a stamp on the back of my hand that was my ticket to gluttony, and stepped inside where the odor of frying onions made me groan with ecstasy.

The cooking was organized on my left and I watched, delighted, as a Jaycee used an industrial-sized spatula with both hands to turn what must have been four or five pounds of sizzling onion rings. Other Jaycees dumped baskets of cut potatoes into vats of boiling oil and patrolled a formation of buns toasting on a ten-foot-wide grill. A grilled bun was mandatory for a hamburger that was truly ne plus ultra.

I joined a line of fishermen heading for a bench covered with butcher paper where the cheeseburgers were served. I was given an extra-wide paper plate that was barely able to handle my gut-buster and outsized ration of potatoes. The potatoes were fried with their skins left on, a sign that civilization, ever on the march, had not bypassed Calamity, Washington.

The gut-buster was deserving of the Jaycee hyperbole, in my opinion, and came loaded with a generous slab of melted cheese; fried onions drooled out of the sides. This was not a sissy burger that you could eat without slopping goo all over yourself; you ate a humongous burger with gusto, snout forward in the manner of swine at the trough.

I poured myself a paper cup of coffee from a stainless steel coffeepot and found an open spot at one of the picnic tables the Jaycees had collected for their enterprise. I had eaten half of my sandwich, gut as yet unbusted but feeling the load, when I heard a commotion outside, with men yelling at one another. The excitement continued; several of the eaters with guts yet intact went outside to have a look. A couple of minutes later, a siren wailed to a stop.

The siren did it. I went outside along with virtually everybody else to see what was going on.

Just off the RV park five or six large boulders sat square in the middle of the Lewis River, and sometime during higher waters two logs had gotten caught on the boulders. Driftwood and debris had collected on the snags until eventually a small island had accumulated.

It was upon this island that a body had gotten caught. The corpse was jammed headfirst under the raft of limbs and logs. Just one foot stuck out, presumably having been spotted by one of the fishermen in the Jaycees' contest.

The siren belonged to a squad car, and a familiar-looking man now stood on shore as three grim-faced deputies, wearing fishermen's chest waders, eased their way out into the white water. I realized the familiar-looking man was Sheriff Starkey. All those billboards hadn't been wasted.

I joined the spectators on the bank as the deputies pulled the body from under the wood.

It was a woman. And she was nude.

And she had been shot in the chest with a shotgun.

Then I saw her face.

Jenny.

I stared dumbfounded.

Jenny MacIvar.

The water was too swift for the deputies to carry the corpse to shore. Instead, they looped a rope under the armpits, and one deputy made his way back to shore with the rope.

On Sheriff Starkey's order the pair in the water set the body free. We all watched as it floated downstream until it reached the end of its tether, then was pulled slowly to the shore in front of the RV park.

When it was about fifteen yards away,

one of the deputies called to Starkey on the shore, 'Whoever it was, took her point-blank, looks like.'

Jenny MacIvar was dead. Murdered.

I couldn't watch any longer. I didn't want to watch them fish her out of the water; I didn't want strangers to see her naked, especially dead. Alive, she had a choice between who saw her naked and who saw her with her clothes on. Now she was at the mercy of the voyeurs gathered at the riverbank. She had flashed her stuff for me in The Dalles, but I knew she wouldn't want me to see her like this.

And I sure as hell didn't want anything to do with watching them stuff her body into the rear of an ambulance; this was the woman who had hopped into my van with her wonderful auburn hair blowing in the wind.

But I couldn't stop myself. I couldn't help it. I glanced back for one more look.

I barely got a glimpse of her as Starkey cleared the way for her body.

Dimples.

That's what I saw, and what I knew

would burn in my memory.

   I wasn't in any mood for my humongous gut-buster, either. I got in my bus and got the hell out of there.

12

The Blues and Boogie Dewlapp

I kicked off my shoes and sank back on the lumpy mattress and propped my head up with the pillow that smelled of mildew. I was tired. My soul, or spirit, or consciousness, or whatever it was that made me what I was, hurt. An existential wound, I suppose is what it was. I ached.

I stared at the sag in the floor, but didn't see it. I could have puked right on the spot. Goddammit to hell, why did this have to happen?

I stared at the sagging floor and saw those long legs of hers as she strode side by side with me into the motel office. She didn't mince along, pretend fluff, like she was being dragged along by some caveman. She was with me all the way. She knew what we were going to do, and she wanted to do it as much as I did. We were partners in this. We both looked forward to it. No pretendsies.

And when I'd discussed our choice of rooms with the clerk, she had joined right in. We both said let's go for it, spring for a room with a view.

I liked it that she wasn't given to logical extremes. She loved the forests as I did, but she understood that a way of life was at stake as well as a species of owl. She was a scientist; her first commitment was to the truth; she simply wanted an accurate count of the owls and a valid description of their requirements for survival.

It didn't make any difference that Jenny had held out on me about her complaints with the wonderful Adonis. The way I looked at it, life was rather like jogging on a private existential trail filled with hazards, on which the end could come without warning, perhaps just around the next bend.

A person meets both friends and louts along the way to the inevitable. I first encountered Willie Prettybird six years ago; our paths having thus crossed, we became friends, he jogging his trail and me jogging mine. He mattered to me, but my concern was not based on how long I had known him; there were assholes that I had bumped into off-and-on for more than thirty years, and I didn't give a damn if I ever set eyes on them again.

I had known Jenny MacIvar just one night, but that had been enough.

And then there were those goddamn dimples of hers. It was the dimples that made me lie there watery-eyed. So what if the wonderful Adonis had had her for fourteen months to my one night? Big deal. He was going to feel it too, but no way could he hurt any more than I did.

In less than an hour Terry and Mary Ellen Harkenrider, accompanied by Boogie's lawyer, Wesley Spooner, having pushed off from Vancouver, would visit me on their way back home. After our talk, the plan was that they would continue on, leaving Spooner behind for a private chat.

I toweled the water off my face and got my emotions under control enough to dial Boogie Dewlapp in Seattle.

His secretary said Mr. Dewlapp was in conference.

'Can you please tell Mr. Dewlapp that I know I am supposed to speak to one of his lawyers and two of his clients this afternoon, but I can't make it. I just cannot take this case. Tell him . . . Tell him . . . Oh, hell, I don't know what to tell him, only I can't make the show this time. Old reliable John cops out.'

Boogie Dewlapp cut in. 'That's okay, Ida, I have it. What's wrong with you, Denson? Tell me what's happened.'

'It's hip, Boog, everything's just fine.'

'Bullshit. Listen to you.'

'Boog . . . ' It was starting to come again. I fought it off.

'Plenty of time.'

He waited while I recovered. I sniffled.

'Okay, tell me what happened.'

'I . . . You see . . . ' I didn't know where to begin. Finally, I made it. One final sniffle, and I knew I would be okay. I took a deep breath and exhaled slowly.

'Atta boy.'

'On the six o'clock news tonight you're

going to hear about how a female scientist for the Fish and Wildlife Service down here to count owls was murdered by a point-blank shotgun blast in her chest. The deal is, Boog, the night before last I helped that woman out when her car broke down in the Columbia River gorge, and that night we had one of life's beautiful moments together. And about forty-five minutes ago, I watched the county sheriff fish her body out of the Lewis River.'

'Bert Starkey. And what do you propose, Denson? To do Starkey's job for him? Elbow the state people out of the way? The law says you have to have a client. You don't. You start poking around in this business on your own, and you can wind up in the slammer yourself.'

'If that happens, it'll be Dewlapp for the defense.'

'Aw, come on, Denson.'

'I either take a shot at doing Starkey's job for him or I hit the trail and get far, far, far away from here, which means I can't handle your Sixkiller case. Dammit,

I'm supposed to be a detective. How could I not try to find the asshole who did that to her? You want to tell me how I could do that, Boogie?'

'Why don't you calm down and get ahold of yourself, Denson? The Harkenrider case is right in the area. Why don't you listen to what the Harkenriders have to say and then make a decision?' I tried to interrupt, but he went right on. 'As a lawyer I have to advise you to keep your nose out of police business, you know that. But keep in mind I'm only hiring you to do a job for me; I have no idea what else you might be doing down there. You're known for your independence as well as your unfortunate preference for screw-top wine.'

Boogie was right, and he was showing a side of himself that those who laughed at his television ads never saw. 'Okay, Boog, I'll listen to what your clients have to say and then make a decision.'

'You've got my card in your wallet, haven't you?'

'Thank you, Boog.'

'I'm sorry what happened.'

'I know you are, man.'

'Whoever it was, find him and bust his ass.'

'I'll do my damnedest.'

13

Secrets of Unexamined Outhouses

They pulled up in front of my cabin almost exactly on time, Wesley Spooner in a polished two-year-old Toyota Corolla, and Terry and Mary Ellen Harkenrider in an aged Chevrolet station wagon with a Skamania-Pacific parking sticker on the window and a faded, barely legible MCGOVERN FOR PRESIDENT sticker on the bumper.

Spooner popped out immediately upon setting his handbrake. He was neatly dressed in suit and tie and carried a fancy leather briefcase. The briefcase had to be a present for his graduation from law school.

About five-six and one-twenty at the outside, he had combed his brown hair into a neat little pompadour and had two outsized, almost beaverish, front teeth. Despite his fancy briefcase and the double Windsor knot on his necktie, Spooner was clearly worried. He chewed on his lower lip as he waited for his clients to join him.

Terry Harkenrider was in his early thirties, slender, with a short beard and curly reddish-brown hair. He wore a headband, faded jeans with a patch on one knee, and a San Francisco Forty-niners T-shirt. Mary Ellen had blue eyes, a quick smile, and medium-length natural blond hair. She had a figure that was an eye-turner; when I was a kid back in Cayuse, they'd have said she was built like a brick outhouse.

After we went through the introductions and handshaking, I ushered them into my musty cabin and poured them coffee. We pulled up folding chairs around the card table, which had a warped cardboard top featuring a fisherman battling an outsized trout.

Mary Ellen took a sip of coffee. 'Fun little cabin you've got here, Mr. Denson. You going to compete in the fishing tournament while you're here? Two more days to go.'

'No, I don't think so. Better to spend my time seeing how I can help you folks out.'

Terry said, 'Jeez, did you hear what happened at Calamity? They fished a woman's body out of the water.'

I ground my teeth together. I had to get them off the subject of Jenny MacIvar in a hurry. 'A scientist here for the owl count, I heard. You folks want to tell me what happened to you?'

'Me, or Mary Ellen?'

'Either one. Take your time. If I have a question, I'll ask.'

'You go ahead, Terry,' Mary Ellen said.

Terry pulled on his beard. 'Well, I drive a Hyster over at Skamania-Pacific, been there eight years, most of which I spent cleaning out the inside of a huge roller. Hotter than the sheriff's pistol in there. Anyway, me and Mary Ellen and the kids went over to my cousin's place at Long Beach to dig clams and fish and collect chanterelles — they're just coming in. I'd worked my way up to three weeks a year, but we decided to come back after two weeks and just mellow out at home. We got back, what day was that, Mary Ellen?'

'Tuesday afternoon.'

'Tuesday. We live in a little house we got rented on the South Fork of Jumpoff Joe. The next day I was out farting around in the yard when Sheriff Starkey pulls up in his squad car.'

'There were four squad cars total,' Mary Ellen said.

'He asked me if he could have a look around, and I said sure, then he gave me these papers signed by a judge saying he had the right. Beats me why he asked me, if he already had the papers. Anyway, he and his deputies made a beeline to a shack Mary Ellen and me have on our place, and out they came, dragging bunches of drying pot plants. Fifty of them. No fucking way Mary Ellen and me grew them on our place. No way.'

'What happened then?'

'He started reading us our rights like we were on a TV show or something and asked us if we wanted to call a lawyer.'

Mary Ellen said, 'We didn't know any lawyer. We've never had a reason to use a lawyer in our lives.'

'Only name I could think of was Boogie Dewlapp from those TV ads of his. So I said, 'What do you think, Mary Ellen, Boogie Dewlapp?''

'I said I didn't know who else to call.'

'So they took you to the jail in Sixkiller and what, gave you a piss test?'

Spooner said, 'They both tested positive, Mr. Denson.'

Terry's face tightened. 'Well, hell yes we tested positive. Mary Ellen and me smoke a joint now and then, big deal. But just because our piss tests positive doesn't mean we're growers.'

'The Boz doesn't require piss checks at the mill, I take it.'

'He wanted to have everybody checked, but the union wouldn't let him get away with it. The new hires have to agree to random piss checks, but I don't have to because I was there before they started that crap. Mary Ellen and me make it from payday to payday, Mr. Denson. I go fishing with my buddies once in a while. My kids and me catch crawdads in the creek. We all gather blackberries in the summer which Mary Ellen makes jam out of.'

Mary Ellen smiled. 'Good jam, too. You drop around some time and I'll show you what I mean.'

'We got a big garden and like to grow things, that's so, but why in the hell would we go and do something stupid like growing all that pot? Do we look like drug dealers? Why are we driving a beat-up old Chevy station wagon that needs tires and a tune-up? It's just ridiculous.'

I gave him a look that said I was sympathetic to his story, which I was.

'The other thing is, it wasn't the best-looking stuff I've ever seen. I'm no expert, but the buds were a trifle on the skimpy side. They could hardly be called buds at all. Pretend-buds is more like it.'

'Mmm. Dinky.'

'That'd cover it. Dinky and full of seeds. I've seen Mexican dirt weed that looked better.'

'Have you ever been involved in a business scheme that went awry, a construction deal that fell through, anything like that?'

'Business? Oh, no. I just like a good nine-to-five-type job. The nights and weekends are for me and my family. I'm just not interested in that type of thing.'

'Outstanding loans?'

'We still owe a hundred and fifty bucks on our VCR, but we'll have that paid off in a couple of months.'

'Tell me, do you always board your windows when you go on vacation?'

Terry said, 'You're damn right, we do. We've been broken into twice in the last three years. You get teenage kids cruising around these country roads, and when they see a house with nobody around, it's a temptation. In town you've got neighbors to keep an eye out for you. If somebody wants to break into our place again, Mary Ellen and me decided to at least make 'em work for it.'

'Anything else I should know?' I always wince when I ask this question. Given their druthers, most people postpone the bad news for last. I've heard horror stories of cancer patients who almost had to arm wrestle their doctors into giving them the full story. Until I forced it out of her, Jenny MacIvar neglected to tell me about the existence of the wonderful St. Adonis who always put the toilet seat down.

Terry looked guilty. 'Well, there is one small thing Mary Ellen and me forgot to tell you, Mr. Spooner.'

Spooner blinked.

I braced myself.

Mary Ellen said, 'We should have told you right off, but you know how it is.'

Spooner said, 'We have to have the whole truth if we're going to be any kind of help.'

'Let's have it,' I said.

Terry sighed. 'Last week Mary Ellen and me let this guy down to work, Billy Akerman, store a couple of his plants in the old outhouse out behind our place. He's got all these relatives going in and out over at his place.'

'Honest, we didn't grow 'em,' Mary Ellen said.

Terry said, 'He'd have maybe laid a few buds on us for lettin' him do it.'

Oh, wow. I couldn't believe it. 'In the outhouse?'

'I forgot all about 'em when we got back from Long Beach. This is Billy Akerman's pot, Mr. Denson, I swear. It doesn't have anything to do with the pot the sheriff found. Billy's not a dealer or anything like that. He just likes his smoke.'

'Billy Akerman. I see.'

'Billy grows weed in a hydroponic system he has set up in a closet in the apartment where he lives, but he got too damn good at it. He's developed these monster buds, but when they get too big and loaded with THC, they start smelling to high heaven. This is what you call skunk weed — it'll knock your head off, but boy does it stink pretty. Hoo boy! Billy's mom is always coming over and stuff so when it gets too smelly he picks it and dries it out in our outhouse.'

I closed my eyes and held them closed for a moment. Figured.

'I moved the outhouse farther back, put it over a new hole Billy dug. We hung his clones under the seat to dry, figuring no cop would want to look down there. But the thing is, when the sheriff drove up, I didn't even think about them. I said, 'Hey, have a look around.' It was after they was all over the place that I remembered, and I just about crapped my pants.'

Spooner said, 'The cops overlooked the outhouse?'

Mary Ellen said, 'I remembered right off, but before I could say anything, Mr. Gracious Host here had invited what looked like the entire sheriff's department onto our property.'

I couldn't help but laugh. 'But nobody looked into the outhouse.'

'At least not down the seat at all the yuck.'

I sighed.

'What do we do now, Mr. Denson?' Mary Ellen was relieved to have the business of Billy Akerman's pot out in the open, but she was still worried.

'You stay away from all pot until we get this mess straightened out. I'll drop by and take care of Billy Akerman's weed. Also I'd like to poke around your place a bit more to see if I can find anything that will help the cause.'

131

Terry looked relieved. 'Just come on by. If we're out to the grocery store or something, you'll find a cement penguin in the front yard. Just tip it to one side, and you'll find the key to the front door underneath.'

★   ★   ★

When Terry and Mary Ellen had gone, I poured more coffee for Wesley Spooner and me. It was Wesley Spooner's turn to solo.

Spooner was on his own — far away from the sonorous Boogie Dewlapp up there in the hurly-burly of Seattle. If you got your start as a lawyer with Boogie, this is what you had to do . . . but at least you got to do it.

A young man and his wife were betting their futures on whatever it was Spooner had learned in law school. I was an old vet, and he respected that. He wanted to prove he was not a nerd. He wanted to win.

'Don't you think these are wonderful cottages, Wesley? Boogie Dewlapp always goes first class, you'll find that out.'

Spooner looked around the room. 'I think they're kind of neat, in the woods and everything. You've got the river across the highway.'

'Good enough for the girls I go with.'

Spooner laughed. 'Me too. My mother always wanted me to be a lawyer. If she could only see me now.'

'So where you from originally, Wesley?'

'Puyallup. My dad ran the produce department of a Safeway there.'

'Lot of veggies on your table at night, I bet.'

Spooner was ready to address the many questions before him. 'Mr. Dewlapp said after I've talked to you, I should hightail it back to our law library in Seattle and give you a chance to investigate. As it stands now, Mr. Dewlapp says no court in the land will convict them for pot stashed two hundred yards up the creek, but he wants all the facts we can get. What do you think, Mr. Denson?'

I liked the Harkenriders and wanted to believe them. I said so.

'I believe them too, Mr. Denson. Would

he have invited the sheriff in knowing he had fifty plants drying in a shack? It doesn't make any difference how far up the creek they were.'

'Not to mention Billy Akerman's hydroponic skunk weed under the outhouse.'

Spooner slumped.

I said, 'The weed the sheriff found was pretty piss poor. Does that matter?'

He gave me an odd look. 'Unfortunately, the law does not adjust sentences according to the quality of the specimen. Marijuana's marijuana.'

'Mmm,' I said. I thought as much. 'These plants may not win blue ribbons but they're still worth a few bucks, right, Wesley?'

Poor Spooner.

'Don't look so gloomy. You've got the makings of a serviceable defense, haven't you? How can the Harkenriders possibly be held responsible for pot stashed that far up the creek?'

'Mr. Dewlapp says I should remember that we're in the middle of a war on drugs. It's impossible to predict anything when you're operating in a climate of hysteria.'

I sat on a folding chair and stared at the throw rug, not seeing it. 'Sheriff Starkey led the raid himself. He was probably extremely careful with the evidence in this case, what with the election coming up and everything.'

Spooner said, 'Oh, yes, Starkey got his name in all the papers — as though he needed it. Have you seen all those billboards of his? They're everywhere.'

'Whether you're Boogie Dewlapp or Sheriff Starkey, advertising's the way to go.'

'Mr. Dewlapp wants me back to Seattle in the morning. You can call me tomorrow afternoon if you like, Mr. Denson.' Spooner chewed on his lower lip. 'I just don't understand this. Jeez!'

I wondered how the Harkenriders would sleep that night, knowing they were being defended by a lawyer who went around saying 'neat' and 'jeez.'

'What do we do now, Mr. Denson? What if Sheriff Starkey should go back there for some reason and find those two plants under the outhouse? That'd be the end of Terry and Mary Ellen. No jury would believe them then.'

'What I do is see to it that that doesn't happen, Wesley. What I do now is go out there and get rid of the things.'

'Isn't that destruction of evidence?' Lectures of his Ethics 101 professor at the University of Puget Sound no doubt raced through his head.

'Naw,' I said, cutting off noble but stupid sentiments. 'Why hell, Wesley, they've got plenty of plants locked up in the sheriff's office. What difference would a couple more make, right?'

'What difference would it make? Let them catch us at it, and then you'll find out.'

'Let them catch me,' I said. 'I'm the one who has to retrieve the damned things.'

What could the poor kid say? I was the old vet, right? Boogie Dewlapp said so.

'Mr. Denson, I want to be up-front about something. This is my very first criminal case. In fact, my first case of any kind, and I don't want to lose it. I want to do right by those people.'

Because of Jenny MacIvar I'd have kept the case even if I thought Terry and Mary Ellen were guilty as hell. But I didn't think that. I agreed with Wesley; I thought the Harkenriders were telling the truth.

'We won't go down without a fight, Wesley. We'll find a way.'

'Thank you, Mr. Denson.'

14

In the Realm of Darth Vader

I couldn't do much for Jenny MacIvar that late on a Friday afternoon so I decided to grab the outhouse pot first, get a good night's sleep, and go to work for Jenny in the morning. I drove to the Harkenrider place, retrieved the key from under the penguin, and took a look around.

I hoped the snooping would give me more of a fix on who the Harkenriders were. If they were the kind of people they had seemed when I talked to them, it was unlikely they were growing fifty marijuana plants.

Shelves of ceramic cows lined the tiny living room, which contained a large Sony television set, a VCR, and a sound system with multiple knobs, switches, and gauges. They were quality machines, but nothing a Skamania-Pacific worker couldn't afford to pay for on time.

The house had two diminutive bedrooms. The master bedroom displayed framed photographs of kids and relatives on a single large dresser, a Mick Jagger poster on one wall, and a floor strewn with dump trucks, dolls, and spaceships. The kids' bedroom contained a bunk bed and a single bed and two dressers; what floor remained was cluttered with race cars and plastic creepy-crawlies and monsters of varying degrees of weirdness. Darth Vader surveyed the litter from a poster on the wall.

The Harkenriders had chosen a poster of Steve Largent of the Seattle Seahawks for the dinette where the family ate its meals. My heart always went out to fans of the Seattle Seahawks, and Largent, the small but slow pass-catching legend, the work ethic in action, was an inspirational choice for the kids.

I wondered if there was anybody in the whole wide world who had a Seattle Mariners poster on their wall. The Chicago Cubs at least got national attention for folding in August or

September. The pathetic Mariners never made it far enough for a collapse to have any drama; the Mariners folded in June and stayed there, poor bastards.

Then, in the bathroom, overlooking the throne, I found a poster of Mike Moore, the Mariners pitcher who had lucked out and gotten traded from baseball purgatory to the Oakland A's, where he won two games in the earthquake World Series with the Giants.

The tour of the house told me what I wanted to know: This was obviously a typical headquarters for big-league dope growers. I'd noticed a Luke Skywalker energy wand and a plastic Uzi on the floor. I was surprised the sheriff hadn't ordered air cover for his raid.

I went out, redeposited the key, and drew myself a little map of the Harkenrider house in relation to the outhouse, the shack, the creek, and the highway, then retrieved Billy Akerman's two plants. I stuffed them inside a black plastic garbage bag before I tossed them into my bus and headed off down the Lucky Buck.

I pulled to the side of the road at a nice sprawl of blackberry bushes. Getting out and collecting the pot, I circled to the side opposite the obvious fisherman's trail through the tangle, and pitched the bag up on the blackberries so it looked like it had been blown there or tossed there by some thoughtless asshole, and had gotten hung up on the thorns. It was easily recoverable with a long stick.

I drove back to Calamity, where I pulled in at the phone booth by the gas station and looked up Akerman, William, in the Sixkiller section. Billy was home and most pleased to be told where he could fetch his weed if he wanted it.

Then I drove a half block to a turnaround above the white water of the Lucky Buck as it swept by Calamity on its way to the Lewis River. Taking my Harkenrider map and a map of Skamania County with me, I walked down to the river's edge and found a flat rock to sit on. I watched a tiny water ouzel hit the water and disappear, swimming under the water.

I had found that if the known facts of a

mystery didn't yield to logic, they almost always yielded to its corollary, the screw-up. The problem with the screw-up, as I'd learned from long experience, was that the logic of disaster changed perversely from bungle to debacle — at least that seemed to be the consensus of prison inmates I'd interviewed during my investigations. The best that a neutral observer of screw-ups could do was lump them into rough groups in order to study what similarities they might contain.

This was my Denson-method Zen detective mode, a version of method acting. To be a Zen detective, you had to put yourself in the shoes of the screwee, that is, act normal. Thus grounded on the bedrock of reality — on Mr. Murphy's law that what can go wrong will — one proceeded cautiously, ruling nothing out of the charmed realm of screwed luck.

Suppose, I told myself, that I, John Denson, signed impossible loan contracts to buy myself a fancy Datsun sports car to impress the women, and a speedboat that I only use a few times a year but justify on the grounds that pussies love it.

But, Keee-rist! I'm up to my ass in debt. I decide the answer is pot. I'll be an in-out drug baron with a patch of fifty marijuana plants planted up here in the woods somewhere — in some sunny, isolated meadow, say.

Suppose I tended those plants from when they were wee sweet babies back in the spring, watering them and keeping them supplied with cowshit, cutting them back, separating males from females, and all the rest.

Now the fall rains have arrived, the nights are getting nippy, and the plants don't look like they're going to get any bigger. The growing season has had it. Harvest time.

I've been planning this all summer, but now I'm getting antsy. This was supposed to be a risk-free, one-time hit: in and out again. I'm spooked about getting caught and don't want to risk doing time. I have to get them in out of the rain and dry them out. Where?

Well, if I work with Terry Harkenrider down at the Sixkiller mill, maybe I see on a bulletin board or overhear at lunch that

Terry is going to Long Beach for three weeks on his vacation. I know he has a shack on his property. I figure, hey, I'll dry my weed in that old shack up the creek from his house. He'll be gone, he won't know the difference.

Nobody will suspect Terry and Mary Ellen Harkenrider. The weed will be safe on their place.

But Terry comes back earlier than I thought. The old wrong-date oopsie is akin to the oh-shit, wrong-time groaner.

But if I'm a mill worker first-time grower, how is it that Sheriff Starkey's anonymous informant knows the pot is there?

I checked my maps again. The business of a North and South Fork of Jumpoff Joe was ripe with possibilities. Any time you have a north-south or east-west anything, the seeds are sown for the old wrong-street — or -highway or -boulevard or -avenue or -road or -trail — screw-up.'

Once, at the Greyhound bus station in Eugene, Oregon, after I'd had a couple too many in the bar next door, I plunged drunkenly into the women's john — your basic wrong-john screw-up — which could be lumped in the same category as wrong floor, wrong apartment, and, alas, wrong bedroom.

Was this a wrong-fork delivery by some stoned would-be pot baron?

15

Condolences to Mr. Northlake

After a sleepless night of tossing and turning, I awoke thinking of Jenny MacIvar peering into the engine of her Volvo that night in the Columbia River gorge.

Minutes earlier I had seen an owl make an eerie appearance in the rest stop above Memaloose Island, the place of the dead. An owl in the dim yellow light floating in the cold wind that whipped up the gorge. Spooky then. More than spooky now.

Jenny said the spotted owl was once called the spectral owl. In the manner of ghosts.

Prophetic, Willie would say. I had to agree.

I saw Jenny again looking up at me from her stalled Volvo. I saw clearly the dimples on her cheeks as she told me about owls and how and where they lived and were tallied. She loved birds and the truth. I liked birds well enough, and I was solidly with her on the matter of truth.

I saw her long thighs in the moonlight spreading to accept me. If Adonis Northlake was so wonderful, why had she done that? If he was so perfect, why hadn't she called him right off when we got to The Dalles? But no, she had jumped in bed with me, laughing and giggling all the way, delighted at the moonlight that flooded down on us from the skylights of our room.

I ground my teeth at the memory of her being retrieved from the Lewis River with a hole blasted in her chest.

She was naked when Starkey's deputies pulled her from the water. Had she undressed for her killer, or had the son of a bitch murdered her, then stripped her corpse?

If it was the former, if she had undressed willingly, then for whom? In spite of my night with her, no, because of it, I didn't believe she was casually promiscuous. This wasn't the Densonian logic at work, more in the manner of a

Prettybird leap of faith, but I knew it was true. Knew it in my guts and heart.

Jenny and Lois Angleton had been sent threatening letters by some asshole who was sore about the owl count. The letter writer had threatened to wring their necks in the manner that the flattened owl had been killed.

Had he changed his mind and switched to a more efficient shotgun? Was it that simple? A deranged logger, sore about spotted owls costing jobs, switching from neck wringing to a more efficient shotgun. I didn't think so, but then you never know.

Also, if it had been a crazed logger, was Lois Angleton next on his list? First one owl counter, then the next.

Or was this a straightforward sex crime? A passing nut or screwball with a sexual imagination gone wrong?

There was something about Adonis she hadn't told me that bothered her deeply. She was upset about his frequent trips to the East, and I still found it difficult to believe that all the environmentalist bucks were back East.

The unabashed, downright ass-kissing enthusiasm of his alleged feminism had made me suspicious of Adonis's character when I met him and Lois Angleton at Delbert's Awful Onion.

I had an assignment from Boogie Dewlapp, yes, and Willie Prettybird. I lived by mysteries. Puzzles had become my life. But no unanswered question had affected me like this.

I got up and took a shower and made myself some coffee and called my best source in Portland.

★   ★   ★

Willie Prettybird and I had investigated several cases in Portland for Olden Dewlapp, and in the course of our work I had come to know Phil Sanford, a hard-core, no-bullshit columnist for the *Oregonian*, himself a former private detective. Phil loved to twist the weenies of crooked cops and amuse his readers with karate chops to public fools, rip-off artists and out-of-control politicians. He had his sources, and I knew he liked me.

I told Phil I was interested in the MacIvar murder. 'This is a personal thing. I knew the lady.'

'Ahh, Galahad Denson.'

'Listen, Phil, I know this is a Washington murder, but I was wondering if the cops in Oregon know any scuttlebutt we're not getting in the news. The killer could be from either side of the river, so they have to be talking to one another.'

'I know a guy who might help. What do you want to know?'

'Anything and everything you can find out.'

'I'll make a call, sure. Take me a few minutes.'

'I'd appreciate it. There'll come a time when I'll pay you back with interest, I swear. I'll give you the makings of a hot column.'

I gave him my number and sat back, unable to take my mind off Jenny being pulled from the water. Twenty minutes later the phone rang. Sanford.

'Well?' I said.

'The cost is a tip for my column if you find anything.'

'Goes without saying, Phil. I owe you one.'

'My source says the autopsy didn't reveal any sign of violence other than the shotgun blast, which drilled her bra and the front of her blouse into her torso.'

'She was murdered, then stripped.'

'That's right.'

'Did they find her clothes?'

'Only the shreds the coroner was able to dig out of her body. The coroner estimated she was dead a couple of hours before she was dumped into the river, but that's not certain.'

'Was there signs of, uh . . . '

'No sex. At least there was no semen that they could find. No pubic hair that shouldn't be there. The cops are speculating she knew the murderer, which is how he was able to blast her straight on like that. The theory is she trusted him, then he whips out a shotgun and bam, before she can react, she's history. If it had been a screwball or a stranger, she would likely have twisted to escape and taken the blast at an angle.'

'A friend then. Or somebody she knew closely.'

'Possibly. But you understand, everything's guesswork at this point, Denson. They don't have anything solid.'

'I take it they're taking a second look at the threatening letters the owl counters received.'

'They are, but they haven't learned squat. Fractured grammar, but you can't conclude much there. That could have been deliberate.'

'Typewriter, printer, or handwritten?'

'Printer.'

'They're not ruling out a pissed-off logger, I take it?'

'No, they're not. Loggers've got computers and printers too.'

'Fuck.'

'Owning a computer is like wearing Nike running shoes, Denson. You've gotta have a computer or you ain't shit. Doesn't make any difference if you never use it. You know that.'

'What about her boyfriend?'

'Oh yeah. Adonis Northlake. Everybody says he's a solid, civilized guy. Their friends all say they were apparently the perfect couple — the good-looking ornithologist and the talented wildlife photographer. Jenny thought he was wonderful, and he's all broken up.'

'I see.'

'Adonis says they were engaged to be married. He burst into tears when they talked to him. Said they were going to have kids and live happily ever after, the whole delusion.'

'He did?'

'Blubbered like a baby. They thought he was never going to calm down.'

'Let me get this straight. Adonis Northlake said he and Jenny MacIvar were engaged to be married?'

'That's right. Said he'd been shopping for an engagement ring. He wanted to get her something real fancy, but he didn't have the bucks. Now he feels like hell. He should have borrowed the money. Denson, you know something the cops don't?'

'Naw. Nothing specific.'

'Don't hold out on me now.'

'I promise, Phil. When I get something

you can use, I'll get on the horn pronto. So you're saying as of now they don't have any kind of short list.'

'They're not ruling anything out. In fact, as my source understands it, they're sending some people along on the recount to protect that other bird woman. What's her name?'

'Lois Angleton.' I took a sip of coffee.

'Angleton, that's it. They wanted her to call off the recount, but she wasn't buying it. She's stubborn as a government mule. Says they're going to count owls as scheduled come hell or high water.'

'What did Angleton have to say? Did your source tell you that?'

'She says Jenny had been distracted in recent months, but she didn't know the reason.'

'Which Adonis attributed to what?'

'Nerves. The usual premarriage jitters.'

'So now what's he doing? Holed up boo-hooing and wearing an all-black Johnny Cash outfit?'

'He told the cops he thinks the killer was an out-of-control logger. He says he was going to photograph the owl count as

154

part of a documentary. The last thing in the world Jenny would want him to do is abandon the job. He's going to see it through in her memory.'

'I see. Well, thank you for your help, Phil. If I get on to something good, I'll give you a call.'

'Sorry I couldn't give you anything more. What's that redskin pal of yours doing these days?'

'Oh, hanging out. Powwowing with his buddies. Doing an occasional job for Olden Dewlapp.'

'Next time you and Willie are in Portland, we'll have a drink.'

I hung up and poured another cup of coffee. Jenny MacIvar sure as hell didn't act like somebody who was about to get engaged. Besides which, engagements and engagement rings weren't her style. She was an intellectual, a nonmaterialist. If she'd married the guy, she'd have worn a simple wedding band, but no stupid, gaudy diamond. Expensive show wasn't her style. She was far too soulful for that.

I wondered what would happen if the cops hooked the blubbering Adonis up to a polygraph and asked him the same questions.

Engagement ring?

Bullshit!

Now what?

I called the St. Helens Motel in Sixkiller and asked to speak to Lois Angleton.

I lucked out; she was in.

I said, 'My name is Richard Chenoweth of Gayle's Jewelry in Portland, Dr. Angleton. I am truly sorry to read about what happened to your colleague. I tried to get in touch with Mr. Northlake to offer him my condolences, but he wasn't in.'

'Thank you, Mr. Chenoweth. Gayle's Jewelry? I'm afraid I don't understand.'

'Yes, isn't it terrible? Mr. Northlake had a diamond engagement ring picked out for Ms. MacIvar, a truly lovely setting.'

A pause.

'Engagement ring?' Her voice was incredulous.

I said, 'Mr. Northlake said he wanted it to be something unique and truly exquisite, so we were custom designing it for him. My heart just fell when I saw on television what had happened to her. She must have been a wonderful woman, so educated, and very good-looking, judging from her picture in the *Oregonian*. These are terrible times, Dr. Angleton.'

'Yes, they are, Mr. Chenoweth.'

'Do offer my condolences to Mr. Northlake, will you? I'm truly sorry about what has happened.' I hung up, leaving Angleton to consider this turn of events.

Sheriff Starkey and the Washington State Patrol might have been taken by Northlake's blubbering, but I wasn't. I knew a liar when I met one, and in my opinion Adonis Northlake lied as easily as most people pour a cup of coffee.

I didn't care how wonderful he was or how good a wildlife photographer. He had not asked Jenny to marry him. I had my man, I was sure of it.

The question in my mind was not who, but why.

Why did he have to kill her?

It was premature for me to go to the

cops with my suspicion. If he had lied this time, he had lied before and would again. It stood to reason that there were lies out there that would pin him, had to be.

Adonis was going ahead with his plan to photograph the owl count for a documentary. I had Boogie's case and Willie's. Plenty of reason to poke around and ask questions. There was no need to hurry. Patience was the thing, and in this matter I had the patience of General Giap. Give me time, and I'd nail that motherfucker and nail him hard.

In the end, justice was all that mattered. Not the swiftness of it, necessarily, but the certainty. If the killer wasn't Adonis, if it was someone else, I'd get him too. I'd been wrong before.

I checked my watch. Time to push off for the parade in Sixkiller.

16

Bubbles from the Gun Turret

I'd promised Willie Prettybird and Donna Cowapoo that I'd try to score an interview with His Famousness Bosley Ellin. The loggers' solidarity parade in Sixkiller seemed a place to start. I didn't want to let the animal people down.

It was a beautiful October day, with a pale yellow sun above the crisp morning air; the leaves were yellowing along the Lucky Buck. It was a perfect day for parades and football games.

It was clear before I got to the bridge that parking was going to be hard to come by on the Sixkiller side of the creek, even though it was only eleven o'clock, so I swung off the side of the road and parked in a packed dirt lot that was no doubt a favorite for high-school neckers and fishermen working the deep hole under the bridge.

I hurried across the bridge and, as though a storm were building, I could hear the thunder and bellow of air horns on the north end of town, and the reply of car horns all over town.

The entrance to Skamania-Pacific was draped with a twenty-foot-wide banner saying: LOGGERS' PROTEST OPEN HOUSE. EVERYBODY WELCOME. In the grounds and yard itself, signs aplenty with arrows directed visitors to the open-house desk, where they might receive a guest tag and a schedule of timber-felling and log-rolling contests, and join one of the many guided tours in which sawyers would demonstrate their skill at reducing a log to a pile of lumber.

I followed a handful of visitors for a crunch-crunch stroll on the graveled path by the pond before I veered off the path of official arrows and went inside the company headquarters.

A young woman was talking on the phone behind the counter, so I checked out the magazines on the coffee table by a sofa that had chrome arms and was upholstered in purplish-red plastic:

People, Sports Illustrated, U.S. News & World Report, Forest Products. That just about covered the spread: gossip to win, news to place, work to show.

In my doctor's office it was *People, Sports Illustrated, Newsweek,* and *Modern Diet* — which offered recipes for brown rice that I never followed because brown rice is such a pain in the rear to cook — but then my doctor was probably far more hip than Bosley Ellin.

The woman with the phone was finished. 'The guest registration desk is straight across the way and to your left. You can't miss it.'

'I'm here to talk to Mr. Ellin, please.'

'Is this about employment, sir?'

'No, it isn't. It's about a professional matter.'

She blinked. 'And you are?'

I gave her my Denson and Prettybird card.

She leaned her head toward a door leading to what I assumed was Ellin's command central or the go-room or whatever it was the Skamania-Pacific cockpit was called. Maybe there was nobody at all in there, but her gesture said otherwise. It said roughly, Sorry, Mr. Curly-haired Man, 'professional matter' won't fly with that unreasonable bitch in there — the bitch no doubt being the Boz's personal secretary, a logical commander of the open house.

The receptionist was on my side, not the unreasonable bitch's. 'And this professional matter is regarding what, Mr. Denson?'

'I'm here on behalf of the animal people to investigate the premeditated murder of a spotted owl on the highway just outside Sixkiller.' I delivered this deadpan, Joe Friday style. 'I'd appreciate your help, ma'am. Spotted owls are an endangered species.'

The receptionist's lips parted slightly. She grinned wickedly. She picked up a pad and pencil and began scribbling.

She looked up with a delightful half smirk. 'And if she asks who these 'animal' people are?' The 'she' was the unreasonable bitch.

I straightened self-righteously, very

formal. 'My clients include Owl, Coyote, Crow, Crawdad, and Worm, among others.'

'She's gonna love this.'

'Some of them are extremely shy and travel only by night,' I said. 'Some live in rivers and others in the mountains. Some live in groups and others are quite solitary. They're quite diverse.'

'Ahh.'

'Elk may be in on this as well, and possibly Panther. Since I'm forced to work through intermediaries, I'm not certain.'

Discretion was her middle name. 'I'll pass this on and we'll see what happens. Mr. Ellin's not in his office, anyway, I can tell you that. It might be a couple of hours before we get our answer back on whether he'll see you. Perhaps you can leave a number where we can reach you.'

I gave her the cabin's number.

Feeling good that I'd given it my best shot, I walked out of the mill grounds and joined the families heading in the direction of Sixkiller's main street — Main Street, aka the highway from Calamity

163

— where a crowd had already gathered. All sit-down space on the curbs had been taken. This did not deter the enthusiasm of the parade watchers. Those who wanted to be guaranteed prime seats had come early, prepared with folding canvas chairs and camp stools.

Main Street was lined with two- and three-story brick buildings that had been constructed in the twenties and thirties, judging from the stolid redbrick architecture. The street ran about eight blocks before it petered out into gas stations and fast-food franchises on the north end of town. In the distance, in the area where the parade was obviously forming, I could see an Arctic Circle and a Dairy Queen.

Parade central was located in the heart of downtown Six-killer, about six blocks from the bridge — downtown being so designated by the dubious honor of having the only traffic light on Main Street. The Evergreen State Bank was on one corner; a True Value hardware store commandeered a second corner; Dixon's Auto Parts occupied a third corner; and

Mr. Lubbock of Lubbock's Fine Furniture peddled his tables and chairs on a fourth.

Gerald Dent, a disc jockey from radio station KFIR in Sixkiller, was the master of ceremonies of the parade — this according to a huge sign on the side of a flatbed truck parked in front of the bank. On the truck Dent, an angular man with a pompadour, was fondling his microphone.

A six-foot-tall white banner with red letters strung across the street above the KFIR truck read: SIXKILLER UNITES FOR JUSTICE AND JOBS.

The television people had parked their vans next to the flatbed truck. KING and KOMO were down from Seattle, and KOIN, KATU and KGW, up from Portland. This was to be a staged event, a staple of television news. The most enthusiastic parade watchers had gathered early, taking up positions near the master of ceremonies and television cameras. Everybody knew all the action would be aimed for the six o'clock news.

Dent said, 'Everybody knows the wise

165

old owl sits up on a limb and asks whoo? whoo? Well, the answer is us, that's who. Folks here in Sixkiller have got their jobs and futures on the line. What we want is a satisfactory answer to why? why?'

Glancing up at the people hanging out of windows, I picked my way through horsey teenagers, women pushing baby buggies, and men with children sitting on their shoulders. I spotted an opening by a trash can about fifteen yards from the television cameras and Gerald Dent's flatbed truck.

From the Dairy Queen end of town, air horns signaled the beginning of the action:

HHHOOONNNK! HHHOOONNNK! HHHOOONNNK!

'And here he comes now!' Dent said, as spectators on both sides of the street rose, applauding for all they were worth, some whistling shrilly.

I didn't know what they were talking about at first; then I saw a man in full logger's getup — boots, suspenders, the works — running up the center of the street from the bridge end of town carrying a shotgun. The cheering rose louder and louder until the logger with the shotgun, having made it into range of the television cameras, dropped to his knees with much drama.

He pointed the gun to the sky and fired off two rounds: *ka-boom, ka-boom*.

And with that two stuffed owls hurtled off the roof of the Evergreen State Bank and landed *splat, splat* on the street, each owl provoking an outburst of applause. I realized the owls were stuffed. Somebody'd thrown them.

The logger scooped up the two stuffed owls, which were each about three feet tall, and from the other end of town, the heralds of air horns sounded:

HHHOOONNNK! HHHOOONNNK! HHHOOONNNK!

'And now, the Sixkiller High School Desperado Band!'

The spectators responded with applause, and the parade was on.

From the northern end of town, I could hear the distant strains of John Philip Sousa's *National Emblem* march. Moments later, a formation of forty or fifty girls led the band into action, each with a holstered plastic squirt gun in the shape of a six-shooter. Their tasseled boots rose and fell in unison as they high-stepped it down main street, waggling their youthful butts and waving green-and-white flags on short staffs.

After the flag girls came the drum major wearing squirt guns on both hips, butts pointed rakishly forward.

As he passed in front of the master of ceremonies and the television cameras, the drum major halted his band, and it went through a complicated drill in which the musicians wove in and out, playing their instruments at the same time. When this was completed, to much applause from the curbs, the band stopped playing and the flag girls faced the cameras. They took their six-shooter squirt guns out and began shooting at imaginary villains, singing a cappella:

> They say, be kind to your night-
>   flying friends,
> For an owl may be somebody's
>   moth-er.

We say, be kind to your wood-
  cutting friends,
For a logger may be somebody's
  fa-ther.

The parade viewers responded with whistles, applause, and blasts from hand-held air horns.

Immediately behind the band, a truck carried logs so large that three was more than a load, and atop the awesome timber a husky logger held high an ax in his right hand and what looked like a flattened owl with his left. He spun the owl by a line around its neck and brandished the ax menacingly.

A banner on the side of the logs said this was Kenny O'Callahan, president of the Sixkiller chapter of the Committee for Loggers' Solidarity.

From his platform, Gerald Dent called out, 'And next, ladies and gentlemen, Kenny O'Callahan with the spotted owl that will be auctioned next Saturday night, in the Hog Wild Saloon in Calamity. We're talking next Saturday night, eight P.M., so there'll be plenty of time to get primed. This is a genuine spotted owl, mashed flat by log trucks. If you want to see the critter before you make a bid, you can find it hanging from the ceiling of the Hog Wild.'

O'Callahan's truck stopped in front of the cameras. He laid the owl on a log, raised the ax high, and brought it down. Not wanting to ruin the prize of the scheduled auction, he just missed the flattened owl, sinking the ax deep into the wood, but everybody got the picture, and the whistling and clapping rose to yet higher decibels.

O'Callahan was followed by a Model A Ford bearing the Honorable Benson Davies, Mayor of Sixkiller, and his wife; they too waved at the cheering crowd.

Then came a cherried-out 1951 Studebaker convertible, carrying the grand marshal of the parade, Mr. Bosley Ellin, and his wife. Ellin was jovial and waved with both hands and with gusto. The master of ceremonies told us that this Studebaker was part of Ellin's personal collection of antique cars that included old Hudsons, Nashes, and Kaiser-Fraziers.

Although I could never afford to maintain one, I admire restored old cars, and the Studebaker was a real beaut in my opinion. So ugly it was grand, evidence of a slightly bent imagination.

The Studebaker was greeted with shouts of 'Atta way, Boz,' 'Give it to 'em, Boz,' and 'Don't let the bastards grind you down, Boz.'

Illigitimi non carborundum, I knew that one well.

The Boz responded to the more fervent exhortations with a raised fist. He reached down and slapped the door of the Studebaker with the palm of his hand, and that was what they wanted to hear: war drums from their fearless point man. Take-no-bullshit Boz would lead them into spirited battle against the legions of the Audubon Society and the Sierra Club.

I probably wouldn't have seen Donna Cowapoo if it hadn't been for the Studebaker. I was following the Studebaker down the street with an admiring eye when I spotted her in the crowd on the far side of the street. She was with an Indian man I had never seen before. Our eyes held momentarily and I gave her a little wave. She smiled and waved back, and then was gone.

I thought momentarily of trying to work my way through the people on my side of the street to see if I couldn't spot her again and then gave it up as a bad idea.

The grand marshal was followed by Miss Skamania County, Ms. Susie Wiggin, a seventeen-year-old senior at Sixkiller High School. Ms. Wiggin wore skintight white trousers and a shirt of sequined white with green trim and waved at the crowd from the back of a Chevrolet convertible, courtesy of Handle's Chevrolet, Vancouver. In addition to being the comeliest young woman in Skamania County, Ms. Wiggin was, as the banner on the door of the Chevrolet informed us, 'a mill worker's daughter.'

Miss Skamania County was followed by members of Posse Diablo, the Sixkiller riding club, and their thirty-eight horses, all prancing and pissing and extruding steaming hot dumplings.

The horse dumplings were scooped up by members of the Sixkiller Elks Club, who wore hip boots and specially crafted baseball hats that featured plastic elk antlers. The scoopers worked in trios: one pushed a grocery cart lined with plastic; a second scooped the manure into the basket with a square-bladed shovel and much pantomime as to the odor that wafted forth; a third honked a bulb horn with each triumphant score.

The truck that followed Posse Diablo carried a log that an inspired chain-saw artist had carved into the likeness of a giant owl. The banner for this truck said: WHAT'LL IT BE, THE SPOTTED OWL OR THE TOWN OF SIXKILLER?

A final log truck was entirely empty. And on the empty bed, a sign said: 'Logs gone to Japan!'

The driver of this truck really leaned into his air horn.

HHHOOONNNK! HHHOOONNNK! HHHOOONNNK!

A squad car from the Sixkiller Police Department brought up the rear, blue light flashing on its rooftop.

Suddenly, a cleverly made mock military tank appeared from a side street and swept around the police car. The tank was fashioned of painted cardboard over a Volkswagen bug. It was a very realistic-looking caricature of a tank, but it had a fir branch for a cannon; someone inside stood in the bug's sun roof and worked the turret from side to side while the driver hit the horn: *meeep, meeep, meeep!* With each *meeep*, colorful bubbles burst forth from the top of the turret.

On the side of the tank a sign read, FRIENDS OF THE EARTH, SAVE THE FORESTS and gave a toll-free number where more information on the state of the nation's trees might be obtained.

The Friends of the Earth tank was met with some good-natured boos and catcalls, but it also received its share of hearty applause, both as a tribute to the brass of the tank driver and his friend in joining the parade, and because the residents of Sixkiller weren't antiforest by any means. They lived in the woods and hunted and fished in them.

The forest was home to them, but it was asking a bit much that they be one-hundred-percenters when their town was threatened with being put out of business.

17

A Quarrel on the North Fork

After the parade was over, I drove down the Lucky Buck to test my hypothesis of wrong-creek screw-up with a little scouting of the North Fork, a slightly smaller branch than the South Fork.

There was a private road on the Sixkiller side of the bridge. There was a house there, too. Only this one had truly long been deserted, and the windows were boarded up as the Harkenriders' had been.

If the wrong-fork screw-up was possible, there would be a cabin or shack off somewhere up the creek. But then, nearly all of these little places had outbuildings one place or other.

Where the road swung away from the creek, there was a turnaround and a trail that followed the creek up into the canyon. That's where I parked my bus, beside a Toyota four-wheel-drive pickup with an aluminum camper on the bed and knobby tires that looked like they were designed for a moon buggy. The owner displayed I LOVE SPOTTED OWLS and SAVE THE WHALES stickers on the front and rear bumpers. I thought the spotted owl sticker was, at a minimum, challenging this close to Sixkiller.

I locked my bus up and set off up the trail, noting that somebody in a knobby-tired rig had tried to drive farther up it. The trail and the creek quickly led into the old-growth Douglas firs that were part of Gifford Pinchot National Forest.

It was a warm day, and I hiked for almost a mile before I found what could, conceivably, support screw-up theory number two: an ancient, rotting cabin with the roof mostly caved in. A sheet of plastic would make it a nice, discreet place to dry marijuana. Just about the ultimate in privacy. A far, far better location than the Harkenriders' shack. One set of feet had been in and out, in and out, several times.

If we were to give any credence to Mr.

Murphy at all, either screw-up was possible: a date screw-up by somebody who worked in the mill with Terry, or a place screw-up by the grower or his deliveryman.

I hustled back to my truck and retrieved my camera and a spray can of Warrenton's, a most wonderful goo. When you sprayed Warrenton's into an impression it quickly hardened into a rubbery plastic that you stripped off like a Band-Aid, thus achieving a soft plastic duplicate of whatever it was that had caused the indentation. This was splendid for pinning miscreants; even saints find it tough to drive a car or walk without touching the ground.

Did those tire prints in the trail belong to the I LOVE SPOTTED OWLS pickup I had seen on the way in? I made molds of those prints and hiked back to the cabin with the broken-in roof. I shot some photographs of the cabin and made some Warrenton molds of the footprints.

I headed back down the trail; a chilly wind lowed in the tops of the ancient Douglas firs, standing as brooding sentinels.

A red-tailed hawk floated high above, riding the wind.

A bone-chilling, translucent fog rolled through the darkening valley and across the fields, enshrouding everything it passed. It tumbled through fences and blackberry bushes; it slid through weeds and past barns and outhouses and over streams; it rushed through trees and ferns and up the path toward me, and then it was over me like I was nothing, and I was alone in a gloom of silence.

On the ridge to my left, an owl went:

Hoo . . . Ho-hoo . . . Hoo.

He had a rich, resonant call. He did it again:

Hoo . . . Ho-hoo . . . Hoo.

Across the small valley, another owl answered:

Hoo . . . Ho-hoo . . . Hoo.

This was a baritone owl, not a tenor or soprano. Hoo, hoo-hoo-hoo, hoo; one, one-two-three, one. I knew it wasn't a great horned; I knew that call. It was my bet this was a spotted.

I cupped the palms of my hands as Willie had taught me, left inside my right, forming a hollow pocket, then spread the knuckles of my thumbs to make a neat mouthpiece. My hands were cold and stiff, but I did my best, sent it right out there:

Hoo . . . Ho-hoo . . . Hoo.

Too high-pitched. John Denson, drag queen owl. I couldn't help but laugh.

A third owl joined the second; this one was King Shit of the Tall Trees, judging from the strength and authority of his call.

Then all three fell silent. They were probably wondering what was happening to the neighborhood. If I practiced and had warm hands, I was confident I could get that call right. Willie would have hit it right on the money, first try, cold hands or not.

I continued on toward my bus. Then, in a field through the gathering mist, I spotted Lois Angleton walking hand in hand with a man.

I had to get off the trail. I angled up to my left through some Douglas firs, running lightly through the underbrush, protecting my face with my elbow. Then I was into the big trees and the ground was carpeted with a pale green moss, a perfect place to hunt for chanterelles; Douglas firs towered above me.

I heard an owl call, but I didn't know for sure whether it was behind me or in front. I vaulted over one dead log, and a second, which was rotten and crumbled under my hand, pitching me onto my face. I scrambled to my feet and hurried through a thicket of ferns.

They were getting near the road; I half ran, half slid down the ridge, keeping the trees between them and me.

The man was in his mid-forties, perhaps, about six feet tall, with an athletic stride. He had a short beard, eyeglasses, and needed a haircut; he wore everything well used: red-checkered shirt, baseball cap, blue jeans, Navy pea jacket, and comfortable-looking old hiking boots.

He talked with his hands, gesturing back at the forest. Then he put his hands to his mouth and made a call:

Hoo . . . Ho-hoo . . . Hoo.

Had that been his call back up the trail? I couldn't tell.

He called again.

Hoo . . . Ho-hoo . . . Hoo.

She embraced him as though he were Gregory Peck going off to war. While they were in the clinch, I sprinted yet closer, ducking for cover behind a large spruce. Now I could see them more clearly, and, once they stopped kissing, could hear bits and phrases of their conversation.

They began arguing. My heavens! So passionate, and now this!

Lois gestured toward my bus. She said something I couldn't hear. I dug my notebook from my hip pocket and started scrawling notes.

The man was louder. 'I tell you, Lois, no harm will come to them.'

Lois murmured something with much emotion. Shaking her head from side to side in anger, she pointed at my bus again.

'Whatever it was she said she saw, he will take care of it. When I tell you he will take care of it, I mean just that. He will. There are ways these things are done.'

She spoke again and mentioned my name. I heard her clearly — or thought I did. Denson, she said. Or did she?

The man lowered his voice and looked her straight in the eye. He was furious. Once he raised his voice: 'Denson.'

I was the subject of the conversation, possibly brought on by the appearance of my bus, which Lois Angleton had obviously recognized. Then they got into his knobby-tired, go-anywhere Toyota pickup and were off, headed toward the Lucky Buck.

I slipped my notebook back into my hip pocket. I heard the *vroom-vroom* of a car starting up on the far side of the turnaround, a noise which sounded suspiciously like that made by the rusted-out muffler on Willie Prettybird's old beater. Sure enough, a junker that looked like Willie's old Dodge Dart went roaring off in pursuit of the pickup.

The start of the owl count was one day away. Had Lois Angleton and Jenny MacIvar located spotted owl nests up this canyon? Counting nests was the first step, Jenny had said.

Was this the place where Lois and Jenny had planned to begin their recount

183

of the owls in Gifford Pinchot? It was my bet that it was.

Lois's use of my name had angered the man. I wondered why? And who was the 'he' they had referred to? I didn't think it was me. Somebody else.

What was it 'he' was going to take care of that would satisfy her?

I reached the turnaround. The tire prints left by the Toyota pickup matched those farther up the creek.

Then I drove to the Harkenrider place on the South Fork and studied the prints there.

Well, well. Unless Lois's boyfriend was a cop, the tire prints didn't all belong to police vehicles. Also, in front of the derelict cabin on the North Fork, I found the distinctive footprints of someone who had been in and out several times. The footprints could have belonged to a cop, but what reason would a cop — or anyone — have for going in and out of a cabin several times if it was empty?

18

The Pain of Mischievous Little Brothers

Maybe it was the weathered log exterior that confidently challenged the worst storm that might whip down from the shoulders of the Cascade range; perhaps it was the fire that cheerily snapped and crackled in the fireplace; or possibly it was the reassuring *ka-klunk, kl-klick, ka-klunk* of ceramic dish hitting stainless steel sink in the kitchen; whatever the reasons, there was something womblike and reassuring about Minnie's Café, now that the pipe was fixed.

The waitress gave me a plastic-coated menu that listed the various specialties of the house: chicken-fried steak; hot turkey sandwich; roast beef au jus, in Calamity meaning with canned beef broth; logger's chili. I ordered a cup of coffee and a bacon, lettuce, and tomato sandwich.

I got my coffee before the BLT, and sat

there wondering if it had been Willie Prettybird's Dodge Dart that had fish-tailed onto the highway after the knobby-tired Toyota.

Darts were unstylish and dumb-looking cars, but they had a good motor, and their dependability was legendary; as their paint oxidized and their bodies rusted, aged Darts went from being good family cars to being good second cars. The rusting hulks that remained would still carry the poor and unemployed, and so a derelict fleet of beat-up Dodge Darts yet cruised rural Oregon and Washington, Willie Prettybird's among them.

I had finished my sandwich and was enjoying another cup of mud when Skamania County Sheriff Bert T. Starkey stepped into Minnie's. He took a seat in an empty booth and ordered coffee.

'Leaded, please. No decaf for me,' he said. A genial man, the sheriff was, ever conscious of people who might vote or have parents who voted.

Starkey looked a trifle heavier — no, a lot heavier — than the photographs plastered on his many political billboards.

Also missing from the billboards were the little pouches under his eyes, no doubt swooshed miraculously away by an airbrush. He even offered the voters hair, perhaps added by a thoughtful artist. Now he sort of had hair; that is, he had thin hair on the sides of his head that he combed neatly over his bald dome. This valiant attempt at youth was frozen with hair spray into neat, hard, shiny furrows.

The sheriff was an extremely fastidious dresser, a trait I have always associated with uptight, authoritarian personalities, as though neatness were somehow associated with political and social righteousness. Creased trousers, correct mind. But my opinion in matters of fashion is suspect, I admit: I regard neckties as hangman's nooses and have Air Denson stenciled on my cheapie, no-brand running shoes; I figure they're all made in South Korea out of the same materials — why subsidize all that national advertising?

Coffee in hand, I followed him to the booth and said, 'Excuse me, Sheriff Starkey. My name is John Denson, and I've been hired by Boogie Dewlapp to help a kid lawyer defend a young couple you busted for having fifty marijuana plants drying in a shack up the creek from their house. I wonder if I might ask you a couple of questions.'

'The Harkenriders.' Starkey bunched up his lips in dismay. 'Won't you have a seat, Mr. Denson?'

'Thank you,' I said, and sat facing him. 'You know, Sheriff, if this kid lawyer of Boogie's has his facts straight, there was just no way in hell you'd ever figure these kids for growing and harvesting that much weed. It's just puzzling as hell, don't you think?'

Starkey took a sip of coffee. 'It is puzzling, I agree, Mr. Denson, but I don't know what I can do other than to proceed according to the law. We found the plants on their property. They have no explanation as to how they got there. They can claim someone put them there without their knowledge if they want, but the law is clear on the matter of my responsibility.'

'How was it again that you came to hit their place?'

'We had heard rumors that somebody was growing pot somewhere between Calamity and Sixkiller, so we planned a sweep to see what we could find. It took us almost two weeks to get everything coordinated, but when we did, we were able to move quickly, and we scored.'

'Lucked out, eh?'

'This is an election year, Mr. Denson. I prefer calling it a combination of good police work and luck.'

I sighed.

Starkey took another sip of coffee. 'Mr. Denson, I assure you that I did not make that bust for political reasons, if that's what you're thinking. We heard the rumors. We planned the sweep. We found the marijuana. We made the arrests. That's what we're paid to do.'

'Yes, I know. That wasn't what I was thinking. I just don't want any kind of miscarriage of justice here. Boogie Dewlapp sends me out on a job, I want to do my best.'

Starkey puffed up his cheeks for a moment, then said, 'I get spooky in an election year, Mr. Denson, I'll have to be honest with you. If you're running for office, one careless word or phrase is all it takes to shoot yourself in the foot, and you're gone, incumbent or no incumbent. Sometimes what you think is the most innocuous, innocent comment imaginable just boomerangs, *ka-plop*, right back in your face like a great big shit pie. Jokes are not allowed.'

'Strikes me as you'd get paranoid after a while.'

'You sure as hell do.'

'Well, then, we shouldn't regard ourselves as opponents. We're both after the same thing.'

He raised an eyebrow.

'The truth,' I said quickly.

Sheriff Starkey raised his rump and retrieved his wallet. 'Of course if you found out anything that would help the state ensure that justice is done, you'd turn it right on over to me first thing, wouldn't you? By the way, is that kid Boogie sent down any good, do you think?'

I shrugged. 'I sure hope so.'

Sheriff Starkey gave me a business card

and finished his cup of coffee. 'If you ever need my help in the cause of truth, you just give me a call, Mr. Denson. I'll do my best to help you out. But right now I'm a very busy man, as you might imagine. I've got a murdered scientist on my hands on the eve of a spotted owl count.'

Did he ever. I wanted to say something but held back and ground my teeth. Dumb, dumb, dumb to let the sheriff know my interest in Jenny MacIvar. Better to let him think I was running around asking questions entirely about the Harkenrider pot. Anything I could get from him I could get more discreetly from Phil Sanford.

Just then the man who had had the argument with Lois Angleton on the North Fork came wheeling into the lot in his Toyota pickup with the knobby tires. The man who had said there would be no problem. *He* would fix it. Whoever *he* was. I said, 'Oh, oh, what is this? An owl lover cometh.'

Sheriff Starkey rolled his eyes. 'Oh, yes, Mr. Denson. In addition to being my little brother.'

Little brother? Well, well.

Little brother appeared not to have been permanently depressed by his quarrel on the North Fork. He was in high spirits as he paused to shoot the bull with a guy who was getting ready to leave the Onion's parking lot.

'You say he's your brother?'

'He's a biology professor at the University of Washington. Mr. Nature Lover. Would you look at that rig? Jesus.'

'I see where he likes his whales.'

'If you went to the parade in Sixkiller, he was the guy operating the turret of the Friends of the Earth tank there at the end.'

I giggled. This was a mischievous little brother.

Starkey sucked air between his two front teeth, a sort of sighing hiss. 'That's not the half of it, Mr. Denson. He directed the study the Audubon Society used for one of its spotted owl lawsuits. There was a big article about it in the local paper, which I sure didn't need, voters behaving as they do. There wasn't a thing I could do except wince.'

'As they say, a free country. I gotta say I have to admire him.' I tried to remember the fragments of conversation I had heard on the North Fork.

Starkey shook his head in sorrow. 'My sister's husband works over at Skamania-Pacific. He said if I wasn't the sheriff of Skamania County, Eric would have been dead long ago. Flattened by a log truck, he says, or dismembered by a chain saw.'

'I can imagine.'

'But it's not as bad as it seems. He would be a liability for me, except the voters all know he managed to get thrown in jail for chaining himself to a crane down at Longview.'

'He got arrested for chaining himself to a crane?'

'He was part of a group of Earth Firsters protesting the shipping of mill-work to Japan. Thank God it was Longview. A friend of mine down there arrested him; I didn't have to.'

Eric Starkey, having said good-bye to his friend outside, clumped into Minnie's. He was a more slender man than his brother and close to ten years younger.

Where the sheriff was solemn and serious-faced — careful as the result of his profession — Eric looked amiable and open.

Starkey said, 'I'm the oldest, he's the youngest. I've always been solid and dependable, straightforward. Responsible is the word. Once married, three kids. But Eric's three times divorced, a bookworm and nature lover. Always pushing me to read Henry David Somebody, about a guy living by a pond.' He shook his head.

'That would be Henry David Thoreau,' I said. '*Walden*.'

'That's it.'

'The name of the pond,' I said.

Eric spotted brother Bert and headed our way, looking pleased. 'By God, would you look here? The women and children are safe now. It's big brother Bert T. Lawman coffeeing up. Hey, Bert! Did you go over to Sixkiller to watch me mow 'em down with my fir branch?'

'Yes, I saw your goofy tank, you damned fool.'

'Bubbles from the gun turret. We even got some cheering, did you hear? I bet we got as much airtime as Bosley Ellin did.

194

They gotta have tape from both sides, right?' Eric's baseball cap featured a neat little spotted owl above the brim, which I thought was nothing short of inflammatory in Calamity.

I stood up and extended my hand. 'Well, it was pleasant talking to you, Sheriff Starkey. I believe I better be running on along now. You know how it is. Places to go. People to talk to.'

The sheriff shook my hand and rose, relieved to be rid of me and my questions. 'Oh, I do indeed know how that is, Mr. Denson. You got anything to tell me, you just give me a ring or drop on by.'

19

Passions of the Hog Wild

That night I decided to check out the Hog Wild Saloon. In a community this small, the local watering hole was the best bet for rumor, leads, and tips.

The Hog Wild had a gravel parking lot around back, where I parked my bus beside a Chevy pickup with a SAVE A LOGGER, EAT AN OWL bumper sticker. I stepped out into a cold, misting rain. The bumper of a Dodge van next to the Chevy asked: HAVE YOU SHOT AN OWL TODAY?

Blowing on my hands, my breath coming in great white clouds, I wound my way through the parked cars to the front of the saloon.

A ten-foot-long WELCOME FEDERAL OWL COUNTERS banner hung over the door in the center of a roofed porch that extended the entire length of the saloon.

The banner would have been neighborly and welcoming except that it was flanked by the same two stuffed owls that had been brought down by shotgun in the parade at Sixkiller.

The inspired owl artist — my bet the wife of a local logger — had started with two pillowcases and made a tuck here and a tuck there, then painted the noble birds in a realistic fashion with carefully applied acrylics, giving them overly large, poignant owl eyes. But the poor birds had hangman's knots cinched very tightly around their necks.

The windows at the Hog Wild Saloon were wet from condensation; Spuds-the-Budweiser-dog stared vacuously out of the filmed-over window on my left, and on my right, Hamm's enthusiastic bear danced atop a shimmering mountain lake. I played the Hamm's song in my head, tom-toms pounding:

In the land of sky blue water
Boom, boom, boom
Land of lofty pines
Boom, boom, boom.

Seen through the film of water on the windows, the patrons of the Hog Wild were indistinct, yet familiar as the figures in Plato's shadow cave. Some were gathered round a potbellied wood stove to soak up the bone-thawing glow of the heat; some sat at the bar watching football on a wall-mounted television set; still others threw darts at a board to one side of the bar.

I grabbed the cool brass handle and stepped inside. I almost did a double take when I saw the flattened owl hanging chest high in front of me. This was the owl that Kenny O'Callahan had mock-executed in the parade at Sixkiller. I took a look at the tag that was tied to the owl's foot:

'This spotted owl, flattened on the highway halfway between Calamity and Sixkiller, was dried and preserved by Kenny O'Callahan and will be auctioned to the highest bidder next Saturday, with the proceeds to go to the Committee for Loggers' Solidarity. There will be a bidding floor of $500.'

Well! Was this bird related to Jenny

MacIvar's missing owl? The Hog Wild was not a franchise bar, as I suppose the flattened owl attested. Whoever owned the saloon had taken some trouble to put together a memorable watering hole.

The walls of the Hog Wild were lined with extraordinary photographs of late-19th-century loggers posed, solemn and stiff-faced, for the man behind the hooded camera. No Union soldier standing before Matthew Brady stood as erect and grand. In one picture, two young men with a crosscut saw stood before a tree that was as wide as three ax handles and a plug of tobacco. In another, a team of scruffy-looking mules — attended by serious-faced men with handlebar mustaches — leaned into their harness to drag a behemoth log out of the woods. A man in calk boots posed on a log floating in a millpond.

Although I knew that the fishermen who stayed at the RV campground must frequent this bar during fishing season, it was clear from the costumes of the customers — filthy boots and baseball caps, heavy-duty jeans, suspenders, flannel shirts and sweatshirts — that this was a logger's hangout in fact as well as decor.

One of the younger loggers had eschewed the traditional gray flannel sweatshirt for one with a stylishly drawn cartoon of a flattened owl with a tire print down its back. Under the owl, the caption read: HOO, HOO, HOO. Another sweatshirt said, IF IT'S HOOTIN', I'M SHOOTIN'.

I wondered where they had gotten such professionally done sweatshirts, but then I noticed that both the tire-print owl and the hootin', shootin' shirts were for sale at the bar in the Hog Wild, with the proceeds going to the Committee for Loggers' Solidarity.

The Hog Wild was one of those places that in the bad old days had featured such bar snacks as pickled Polish sausage — vinegared fat sticks that would have made an actual Pole vomit — and pickled eggs and jerky and peanuts and chintzy little bags of Cheetos and Fritos; those goodies, in the age of the microwave, had been replaced by such exotic fare as frozen pizza and Poor Boys, freshly zappable on the premises.

I was pleased to see a large jar of pickled eggs behind the bar, perhaps a gesture to the old farts who frequented the place. I took a stool and ordered a Rainier draft and a couple of the eggs, aware that I was close to being the only nonlogger in the place. I was almost certainly the only nonlogger to order a pickled egg.

In the dime novels it had been the ranchers versus the sheep men; in these parts it was down to timber cutters versus owl lovers and not a lot in the way of tweenies.

In other parts of the country, an Irish walking hat might qualify as the affectation of an intellectual in the tweedy, fuddy-duddy academic tradition and thus of someone out of touch with reality, that is, with such plebeian concerns as jobs and paychecks — but not in Calamity, Washington. As the males living west of the Cascades knew well, an all-wool Irish hat was perfect for misty rain and a dandy place to store flies; it was my bet there were more men wearing those hats in western Oregon and western Washington and British Columbia than in all of Ireland. An Irish walking hat was functional, which was why it was a classic in both Calamity and Cork.

I could have simply been a fisherman down from Seattle — confused as to the quarrel between loggers and owl lovers and indifferent to the plight of either — here to willingly freeze my ass off in a manly, if masochistic, search for the elusive steelhead.

Judging from snatches of conversation I heard as I ate one of my eggs, football was hardly the biggest concern in the Hog Wild — even to those who were watching it. Besides, the spectacular plays — sacks, interceptions, gross screw-ups, hard hits, outrageous catches, and touchdowns — would be replayed for those fans who had gone to take a leak.

The man next to me sported handsome muttonchop sideburns and wore a heavy sweater over a long-sleeved checkered shirt. His bearded friend wore a Bardahl Motor Additive baseball cap.

Muttonchops said, 'You can hold all

the parades in front of all the fuckin' television cameras you want, but the real question is what difference does it make whether they find any owls or not? None of this bullshit ever had anything to do with owls and everybody knows it. It's trees. Well, shit, it ain't even that.'

'It ain't?' Bardahl said.

'Gorbachev took away the fuckin' bad guys, but people still want villains. They can't live without 'em. A man don't need a P-h-fucking-D to figure that out. First thing you know they'll run some poor logger up on charges of murdering that woman they pulled out of the river.'

'The birds are out there, don't tell me they ain't,' Bardahl said. 'Every time they go out there they find more birds. Now just how in the hell does that happen, I ask you?'

Muttonchops shook his head, his face tight. 'I wouldn't put it past the Audubon sons of bitches to send nature lovers with shotguns after them owls just so they could piss and moan about how it was because of the loss of their precious goddamn forest. Habitat, they fuckin' call it. Jesus H. Christ! I'm getting so I can't stand that goddamn word. Them owls sleep all day. Who the hell cares if they got squirrels to eat? You tell me. It ain't like a deer. At least a man can eat a deer.'

Bardahl laughed. 'Great horned owls'd do it. They say in the papers where a great horn'll eat them fuckin' little spotteds like they was popcorn.'

'What do you want me and the old lady to bring next week?'

'Your worthless hides and maybe a six-pack. We'll boil hot dogs for the kids and load 'em up with chips and potato salad.'

Muttonchops laughed. 'We'll send 'em outside to see how many take leaks in poison oak. Did I tell you what happened to Danny?'

'Oh, no! Poison oak?'

'Got it all over his damned pecker. His buddies on the soccer team all laughed their asses off in the shower after practice. Poor damned kid.' Muttonchops giggled. 'I had a heart-to-heart with him, you know, real father and son stuff. I said, 'Danny, now dammit, you're going to have to learn where you can put that thing and where you can't. You just can't stick it into any old bush.'

Bardahl laughed. 'I'll have to razz his ass. God, can you imagine getting that stuff on your dick.'

Beer in hand, I drifted over to a couple of notices on the wall to see what the local action was.

A neatly printed poster said the spotted owls hanging on the porch would be auctioned off at the annual Christmas dinner given for the employees of Skamania-Pacific's plywood mill — the proceeds going to the Committee for Loggers' Solidarity.

Next to the notice of the owl auction, a sign-up sheet gave the full poop about an 'air horn honk-in' scheduled for the following Friday when the odious owl counters ate dinner at Spanarkle's Restaurant in Sixkiller after their first week in the woods.

The notice said the 'symbolically empty' log trucks would meet at Calamity at four P.M.; from there they would travel by caravan to Sixkiller, blowing their 'air horns of resistance' along the way.

If you didn't have a truck with an air horn, you were invited to follow behind the big honkers and blow whatever horn you could come up with. If you really wanted to support the cause you could buy a fifteen-dollar I GIVE A HONK FOR LOGGERS T-shirt.

The various announcements and pronouncements of the solidarity committee — including a bulletin board reminder of the auction of the flattened owl — were signed with Hancockian boldness by Kenny O'Callahan, president of the Sixkiller chapter of the Committee for Logger's Solidarity, the obvious Lech Walesa of Sixkiller.

O'Callahan didn't have his heart set on a modest auction. He had sent invitations all over Oregon and Washington, and, judging from a posted list of people saying they would attend and enter bids, the response was terrific.

I counted twenty-seven out-of-town acceptances, and I bet the number was growing. In Washington, those who had said yes ranged from the owner of the colorfully named Dinky Outfit Inc. of Forks, on the Olympic Peninsula, to owners from Enum-claw and Mossyrock in the Cascades. Solidarity Committee loggers were coming from Sno-homish and Snoqualmie to enter bids for the owl. Oregon was solidly represented with mill owners or loggers from Clacka-mas in northern Oregon, just outside Mount Hood National Forest, to Brookings at the edge of the Siskiyou National Forest in the extreme southwest.

I had to hand it to O'Callahan. The auctioning of a flattened spotted owl to loggers from both states promised to be quite a media happening.

The gang around the stove was talking about owls, and so, too, were the duo at the dart board playing 301. I moved down the bar to watch and listen to the dart players.

Ron, a slender young man with curly red hair and a Committee for Loggers' Solidarity T-shirt, toed the line with a well-used boot. He was sitting on an 83, which meant he wanted a triple-17.

As he eyed the triple-17, his opponent, wearing a yellow Caterpillar tractor baseball cap, said, 'You know, what Kenny ought to do is train them Harrises of his to hit great horneds. They could do it, couldn't they? A Harris hawk one-on-one against a great horned.'

Ron let fly. Single 17. 'Aw, screw!' he said.

Caterpillar cap held his left fist up to represent the target great horned owl, spread the fingers of his right hand and held it high to represent the Harris hawk, and *bap!* grabbed his fist with his hand. 'Harris zaps 'em. Little aerial action there. We could make side bets.'

Ron frowned at his miss. 'Bet it'd be a battle,' he said.

It was Caterpillar's turn, and he was sitting on a 40. He snapped his finger. 'Double-top for the winner. No problem with this one. This's my number.'

'Shit too,' Ron said.

Caterpillar took a deep breath and let it out, concentrating on the top of the board. He stroked the winner with a neat *thup!* of the dart.

Which is when the grinning Kenny O'Callahan made his entrance into the

Hog Wild, accepting celebratory hand-shakes from his friends. He said, 'I would have been here a hell of a lot earlier, but I had to sit the kids while the old lady finished her watercolor class.'

The Great Protester had sinewy shoulders that bulged with the power of redwood burls. His curly hair was so black and his skin so white that he was doomed to eternal five o'clock shadow; I couldn't imagine he ever looked truly clean-shaven. He wore a long-sleeved wool shirt and blue jeans held in place by wide leather suspenders; the suspenders denoted lumberman in Calamity, Washington, just as a wide-brimmed hat with a sweat-soaked headband and jeans with flakes of dried manure on the cuffs was the designated cowboy costume in Pendleton, Oregon. This getup was not unlike that O'Callahan had worn in the parade at Sixkiller, and I'd bet dollar bills against dingleberries that he wore one like it everywhere he went.

After a couple of minutes of recounting the parade he pulled out a set of darts and joined Ron and Caterpillar.

I took a seat near the board, hoping for an invitation to join them. Partners were generally preferred to three players.

Ron glanced my way. 'You play darts?'

'I know what a breakfast is,' I said. A breakfast was a score of 26 in darter's lingo.

'You probably know what a ton-80 is too,' he said. 'Would you like to join us for a game of doubles? None of us are very good.'

'Sure,' I said. A ton-80 was three trip-20s, as good as you could get. I offered him my hand. 'John Denson.'

I was introduced to the man with the Caterpillar cap, whose name was Charlie, and to Kenny O'Callahan.

Ron handed me a dart. 'Shall we cork for partners?'

'Sure,' I said. I concentrated on the bull's-eye. I knew about good form. I knew how it was supposed to be done. I concentrated on a tiny spot on the bull's surface. I kept my elbow under my hand and not sticking out like a chicken's wing. I did all of those things.

I let fly, remembering at the last second

to follow through.

Wide and six inches to the left. My textbook follow-through looked pretty silly with a miss like that, but I lucked out; I was widest, Kenny O'Callahan closest, so we were partners. Kenny corked for the start and lost.

While he was waiting to start the play for our side, I gave him a Denson and Prettybird card. 'I'm trying to find the folks who stashed weed on Terry and Mary Harkenrider's place. You must know them. You don't believe for a second that they were growing fifty plants, do you?'

O'Callahan kept his eyes on the board.

I said, 'I've been wondering how come it was the sheriff chose to land on that particular place at that particular time.'

'They're getting stiffed by somebody,' O'Callahan said, still watching the board.

'The sheriff told me he'd been planning a search of that area for a couple of weeks.'

'He told the newspaper people the same thing.' O'Callahan took his turn on the line. We were playing double-on, double-off, and he had to hit the outer ring to get us started. He hit the double-16, first dart, and we were away.

I waited until he finished his turn before I continued. 'What if he knew the pot was there all along?'

O'Callahan liked that kind of talk. 'Terry and Mary Ellen ain't growing no fifty plants. That's horseshit.'

I said, 'You know, on the subject of all this talk about owls, I took a little hike up the North Fork of Jumpoff Joe today, and I heard some owls up there. That's where they're going to count them tomorrow, isn't it?'

'What did they sound like?'

I rubbed my hands together and blew on them. 'Just a sec. Okay, are you ready?'

'Give it to me.'

'*Hoo . . . hoo-hoo-hoo . . . .hooo.*'

'Once more.'

'*Hoo . . . hoo-hoo-hoo . . . .hooo.* Well, what do you think?'

O'Callahan laughed. 'Better stay out of a spotted owl gay bar sounding like that.'

Charlie said, 'Speaking of staying out of places. Have you been hearing stories about a big cat screaming at night over on the North Fork of Jumpoff Joe?'

'A panther?'

'That's what they were saying at the feed store over in Sixkiller.'

O'Callahan said, 'Aw, that's just bullshit to scare the owl counters.'

'I only know what they're saying. I heard two guys say it. A mountain lion on the North Fork. One said its scream was the damnedest thing he'd ever heard. Gave him the willies.'

20

In Fields of Plenty

Sunday morning. The big day. Owl day. The questions remained: Who murdered Jenny MacIvar? Who killed the spotted owl? Why?

I ate a breakfast of cornflakes and coffee in my cabin, wondering if the Harkenriders were back in their place on the South Fork and if they had thought of anything that might be useful to me. I tried their number, and it was busy. They were home so I fired up my bus.

About halfway between Calamity and the Harkenrider house, I spotted the Harkenriders' station wagon parked off the road. They were picking pumpkins in a patch down by the creek.

I pulled over and parked beside their wagon.

The pumpkin patch was part of a larger garden that had mostly been harvested.

To get there, a person had to part two sagging strands of barbed wire and ease his way through, watching for snags, and then hike across a pasture still sodden from the previous night's rain.

The trail through the field was outright mud slime, so I tried the grass. Like a damned fool, I started out thinking I could make it without soaked feet, and of course the field was sodden, and naturally, *yecchhhh*, my left shoe leaked, and my sock was instantly wet. One step later, my right shoe went, and from then on it was yuckosville with each wet step.

I persevered, squish, squish, through the slime and goo.

The main thing I had to watch out for were cow pies. Dry pies were a light sandpaper color and you could see them okay, but when they were freshly bloated with rain they turned an insidious greenish brown color that blended right in with the grass and mud.

There were more than a couple of pies in the field; in fact it was covered with them, some real beauts — Lake Titicacas of wet shit without so much as a dry film on top. Careless flies and errant bugs perished in these unexpected pits like the dinosaurs at La Brea. I dodged several wicked numbers with nifty moves; I didn't want to make my entrance skidding casually on my back.

Terry and Mary Ellen looked up from the pumpkins and waited for me.

'Hon, it's Mr. Denson!' Terry looked pleased.

'Hey, how're you two doing?' I called.

Mary Ellen was all smiles. 'We're doing fine. It's taken us a while to get calmed down after the shock of it all, but we know we didn't do anything wrong and the truth will come out. We're feeling better about it.'

I held my hand out as I got near Terry, risking a last-second misstep by taking my eyes off the pasture in front of me. 'Wonderful-looking pumpkins.' I made it without incident.

Mary Ellen said, 'Have you found anything that could help us out, Mr. Denson?'

'Well, I don't know for sure. I ditched that weed for you while you were down in

Vancouver, but that's about it.'

'Billy phoned to thank the masked man who gave him the call. Thank you very much, Mr. Denson. We appreciate it.'

'No biggie. Say, there's a question that's on my mind, but I forgot to ask it at my place the other day. Have you had any of those federal owl counters around here in the last few weeks?'

Terry said, 'Oh, sure. A couple of real nice ladies in a fancy rig that was like an RV remodeled into a laboratory. But you know something, Mr. Denson? One of those women was that lady they found floating in the Lewis River.'

'Her name was MacIvar.'

'That's it. Jenny,' Mary Ellen said. 'She had long auburn hair, I remember. Beautiful hair.'

I thought: Please, for Christ's sake, don't mention dimples, Mary Ellen.

Terry said, 'If you drive half a mile up the creek here you'll see a dinky feeder creek on the left that empties out of a steep little canyon. That canyon winds way up in the mountains.'

'They were counting owl nests,' Mary

Ellen said. 'Found a couple up there and three more one canyon over.'

'The North Fork,' I said.

'They didn't like to leave their vehicle around with nobody to watch it, so they asked us if they could park it at our place. They were in and out of here six or eight times.'

'Say, our bust doesn't have anything to do with the murder of that lady, does it, Mr. Denson?'

I was wondering that myself. My money was still on Adonis Northlake, but I couldn't overlook the mysterious conversation between Lois Angleton and Eric Starkey on the North Fork. Had Jenny seen something fatal on one of her forays into owl territory? I said, 'Oh, I don't know, Terry. I kind of doubt it. Did those women mention seeing anybody with pot when they were hiking up into these hills?'

Terry thought about that for a moment. 'I can see what you're getting at. Unfortunately, no, they didn't.'

'Hmm. Has either one of you seen anything peculiar going on in the woods around here?'

'I can't think of anything,' Terry said.

'How about you, Mary Ellen?'

Mary Ellen said, 'Not unless you count the guys with the spotlight.'

'Oh, hell yes, forgot all about that. The guys with the flashlights or spotlights or whatever. We seen 'em one night coming back from Mary Ellen's mom's, and two nights later Mary Ellen's brother seen 'em when he was coming home from work. They was one canyon over from this one.'

'That'd be the North Fork again.'

'We could see 'em from the highway.'

'What were they looking for, do you think?'

'It beat hell out of us, didn't it, Mary Ellen? Deer poachers don't go out there in that thick timber, man, they cruise the roads. Besides, they had their beams aimed high up in the trees.'

I said, 'Maybe it was people counting the spotted owls, or getting ready to.'

'Say, that's it. I bet that was it, don't you think, hon?'

'Had to be,' Mary Ellen said. 'The article in the paper said they flash lights in the trees to catch the eyes of spotted owls. It was probably the two women that parked their rig here. I'd bet on it.'

I said, 'Say, you don't know of any locals who really know their stuff about owls? Maybe a bird-watcher or somebody?'

Terry scratched his chin while he thought it over. 'I don't know. Owls?' He laughed. 'You want to know a guy who's into owls?'

'Kenny O'Callahan,' Mary Ellen said.

Terry said, 'Well, yes, Kenny. This guy down at work, Kenny O'Callahan, has got himself a pair of Harris hawks trained to hunt. He's got these leather gloves and hoods and stuff. It's really interesting.'

Mary Ellen said, 'You might have seen him in the parade at Sixkiller yesterday. He was the guy with the ax and the flattened owl.'

'Kenny O'Callahan just hates them fuckin' Auduboners and Sierra Clubbers. For a while he was all excited about getting himself a pair of spotted owls from a guy in northern California somewhere.'

'Eureka, hon.'

Terry said, 'That's the place. Eureka, California. Anyway, one day down at work, he was all excited telling people how he was going to use them as targets for a mill workers' benefit. He told Ellin about his idea, and the Boz said he could store them at that fancy retreat of his up the South Fork. He's got a big barn up there where he keeps his antique cars. Plenty of room for them to fly around and stuff.'

'Up the road from your place.'

'That's it. Kenny called it something. What was that, an aviary, hon?'

'Something like that.'

'What happened to the idea?'

'I think it was just a lot of bullshit. Kenny mentioned it once and that was it. If it wasn't bullshit, he'd have been giving us all the details. I'd forgotten all about it until you mentioned owls just now.'

'But he did manage to lay his hands on the flattened spotted owl the solidarity committee's going to auction.'

'Oh, yeah, that was his doing. They got

it hanging down in the Hog Wild Saloon in Calamity.'

'Callahan's not into weed, I don't suppose.'

'Kenny? Naw. Kenny might take a hit on a joint now and then, I don't know. Both of us were there before the Boz started random piss checks on new workers, so we don't have to worry about it. One thing's sure: Kenny ain't growing no fifty plants. Jeez!'

Mary Ellen shook her head. 'That's big-time stuff, and he's got three little kids, same as us.'

I said, 'If you want I could lug a couple of pumpkins on my way back. Help you out a little.'

'Sure, Mr. Denson. Save one of us an extra trip. This guy down at Calamity lets us use this little piece of land for nothing. All set up for irrigation and everything, but it was overgrown with blackberries; he said if we had that much energy, go ahead and cut the bastards down and put in a garden here if we wanted.'

'We load him up whenever anything comes in. This is pumpkin time.'

'I bet you have a freezer full of good grub.'

'Oh, hell, yes,' Terry said.

'Let's have 'em then,' I said. They loaded me up with a huge pumpkin in the crook of each arm, and they took two pumpkins apiece. We set off through the mud, balancing our loads and watching for shit slicks. If this wasn't exactly negotiating the land mines of life, it was close.

We had gone about ten yards when Mary Ellen avoided a plop of excrement with a particularly agile side step.

'Atta girl,' Terry said.

'Nifty move, Mary Ellen.' In saying that, I stepped back to adjust my load of pumpkins and stepped in something that yielded suspiciously. '*Ahhhhhhhhhhhhh!*'

'Oh, my God!' Mary Ellen said.

'Shit!' I said, disgusted.

Terry laughed. 'Shit is just exactly what it is.'

I lifted my right foot out of the pile of gooey yuck and did my best to wipe the mess off on the wet grass, wondering if this was some kind of omen for the day.

'Just be glad you don't have to use that grass for toilet paper,' Terry said.

I got the yuck off the best I could, knowing I was going to have to put my shoe under a hose when I got back. I ignored the weight of the pumpkins and carefully considered each step. For example, clumps of grass signaled potential disaster and were to be avoided. I regarded each clump, each off-color patch with maximum suspicion.

Thus on the alert, I managed to make it to the barbed wire without any more missteps and without dropping a pumpkin. Terry Harkenrider put his pumpkins down and swung his arms to relieve his stiff shoulders. He held the strands of wire apart for me to go through.

'Go on ahead, Mr. Denson.'

Thus awarded the honor of going first — and stupidly holding on to my pumpkins instead of setting them down so they could be passed through — I stooped to ease between the two strands of wire. I was halfway through, Cool John, when the left pumpkin started to slip, and I turned to get a better grip on it . . .

. . . and caught a barb in my crotch.

'Aaaahhh!'

I straightened and hit the top wire.

Terry and Mary Ellen, both laughing, relieved me of my pumpkins so I could check myself for damage.

Shaking with laughter, Terry said, 'Stepped in cowshit and snagged his balls in one trip out of a pumpkin patch. You see, hon, this demonstrates the quality of private investigator Boogie Dewlapp sends to Sixkiller to help keep us out of jail. Boogie told us: He hires nothing but the best.'

* * *

It occurred to me as I drove back to my cabin that surely Terry and Mary Ellen, who had grown two splendid gardens the previous summer, would almost certainly have produced some decent buds if they'd decided to dabble in the marijuana trade.

They surely wouldn't have wound up

with buds of the nature confiscated by Sheriff Starkey.

It was also interesting to learn from the Harkenriders that Jenny and Lois had been up and down both forks of Jumpoff Joe six or eight times scouting out spotted owl nests. Plenty of opportunity for one of them to see something she wasn't meant to see.

Then I had the passionate Mr. O'Callahan and talk of stockpiling owls.

I pulled to the side of the road and retrieved my notebook from the glove compartment. I flipped through my scrawls until I found the heated conversation between Lois Angleton and Eric Starkey on the North Fork:

Wn pts at my bs

Mn I tel yu, Lois, no hrm wil cme to thm

Wn — angry, cn't hr

Mn I knw wht sh sw. H wil tke cre of it. Whn I tel yu h wil tke cre of it, I mn jst tht. He wil. Thr r wys thse thngs r dn

No harm will come to them. No harm will come to whom? Terry and Mary Ellen?

I know what she saw.
Who saw? Jenny MacIvar?
Saw what? The man with the marijuana?
And who was *he*?
He will take care of it. There are ways these things are done.
The man talking was the sheriff's brother. Was he talking about Sheriff Bert Starkey? Bert Starkey could help the Harkenriders if he put his mind to it.
I grabbed myself a six-pack of Rainier at the Mini-Mart and headed for my cabin. I opened my door, went barging inside, and heard a woman say, 'Hello, John,' as I slipped the beer into the refrigerator.
I turned to find Donna Cowapoo peering around the bathroom door, her head a froth of shampoo suds.
She said, 'I came over with Willie a while ago. Bosley Ellin's secretary called to say he'll be at the Sixkiller Hot Springs this afternoon between three and four, and if you'd like to talk to him, you ask the woman at the desk. Willie and I thought it might be fun if I went with you.'

'I don't see why not.'

'Oh, good. Thank you. I hope you don't mind that I'm using your shower.'

'Boogie Dewlapp's springing for the hot water.'

'I was with some friends at the parade or I would have come across to say hello.'

'I thought that might be the situation.'

'That was it. Be right back. Just a sec.' Donna's soapy head disappeared.

I started heating water for a cup of coffee before we left.

From inside the bathroom, Donna called, 'I'm not making us late, am I?'

I checked my watch. Two o'clock. 'Plenty of time.'

21

In the Hall of Tubs

Jenny MacIvar was two days dead, and I was making little progress, except that I was positive — I'd call it gut instinct if I had any — that Terry and Mary Ellen Harkenrider's misfortune was tied to her murder.

And the start of the owl recount was eight hours away. If I couldn't make some progress in finding Jenny's killer, I had an awful feeling another owl counter might die. One thing was sure, whoever it was who had wasted Jenny with a shotgun was somebody dangerously out of control.

And what of the owl killer — the person who'd delicately, forcefully wrung an owl's neck? My clients the animal people might not be too forgiving if I didn't find something soon. Besides, I was convinced that the killing of bird and woman were also connected, although I

229

was as yet miserably unaware of exactly how.

As I set out with Donna Cowapoo to interview Bosley Ellin, I was borderline numb from trying to figure the connections.

The Sixkiller Hot Springs contained a bare-ass side and a sissy-prude side. I hoped fervently that Bosley had gone for civilized bare ass; maybe the sight of Donna Cowapoo would stiffen his nu-nu and loosen him up.

As I understood it, the name Sixkiller was applied to the hot springs long before the logging settlement of the same name was established on the Lucky Buck. The story was that six horse thieves had been shot in ambush while soaking their tired bones in the hot water.

Soon after we passed the turnoff to the Harkenrider place, the road wound higher into the Douglas firs, and the awesome trees — in this case eighty or ninety feet high — rose in primal splendor on either side of the road.

I said, 'You know, that woman Jenny MacIvar said some of the trees the government proposed to cut were six hundred years old or more. A tree that old would have been a seedling in um . . . ?'

'The fourteenth century.'

'Shakespeare wrote his plays in — what — sixteen something? What the hell was going on in the fourteenth century? Charlemagne? The Crusades? A plague of some sort?'

We rode in silence for a half mile.

Finally, Donna said, 'You know, John, it strikes me that the citizens of a right-thinking republic could do worse than be buried under trees.'

'I agree. Nonwasteful. Recycle everything.'

'At a commemorative service, somebody'd plant a seedling of your choice six inches above your belly button. When the roots sucked up whatever minerals from your body it needed for a healthy start, you'd rise with it and feel the wind and seasons in its branches.'

'I see. Existential compost. And suffer the tree's risks of drought, disease, and the lumberman's ax.'

'That, too.'

'Juniper for me, I think.'

'Why is that?'

'Well, I read somewhere that they live a long time, and their berries are used to flavor gin. I want a contemplative landscape and a ready whiff of gin when the summers get hot.'

'I'll be a cottonwood. I'll have mushrooms pop up at my feet every spring like so many children.'

I slowed the bus and checked the speedometer. We were at the main branch of Jumpoff Joe — before it split into the South Fork and North Fork.

It was four miles from the Harkenrider place. A half mile past the fork of the creek, and we were there; the hot springs welled up from the side of a heavily timbered ridge about a hundred yards from the creek.

The hotel at the hot springs featured a thirty-foot-tall façade in the manner of saloons and whorehouses in old cowboy movies, and a porch about fifteen feet deep and maybe sixty feet wide, which had to be ideal for contemplative rocking in the afternoon.

I pulled into the parking lot and said, 'Well, what do you think, Donna?'

She grinned. 'It's beautiful. I sort of hope he chooses the no-clothes side. Willie'd just love that.'

As we walked, her little butt went this way and that in a manner most fetching. I agreed with Willie.

She caught my eye and said, 'You've seen a woman's rump before, I'm sure. Behave yourself.'

'I don't know if I can.'

'You can't if you don't try.'

We stopped on the porch to read a plaque that said a small hotel had been built at the hot springs in 1896, but burned in February 1912. The current hotel had been built in 1918. A map of the hotel showed three wings of custom-made porcelain tubs in the back; the handsome tubs were made by German craftsmen in St. Louis.

We stepped through heavy wooden doors — upon which bears had been carved in relief — into a lobby that smelled musty and woodsy and old.

The receptionist, a pleasant-looking woman in her early seventies, wore a brown hairnet over her blue hair and was listening to rock and roll from KFIR in Sixkiller; her eyeglasses had unusual plastic rims featuring what looked like Batman wings highlighted by flecks of gold sparkle.

I admired the stuffed elk's head over her desk, although its glass eyes needed dusting. Trying not to be distracted by the Batman wings, I said, 'My name is John Denson. I have an appointment to chat with Mr. Bosley Ellin at three o'clock.'

'Oh, yes. Mr. Denson. Mr. Ellin is expecting you.' The receptionist was trying not to be distracted by Donna Cowapoo.

'He's been having a good soak, I take it.'

The receptionist smiled weakly. 'Mr. Ellin has had a nice long soak this afternoon.'

'He's a busy man. The hot water is probably good for him.'

'Mr. Ellin is a regular here. He loves his hot water. He has an estate just up the road a couple of miles. He says he built it there because it was so close to the springs. You'll find him in tub seventeen, Mr. Denson. Eh, Mr. Denson, will you be taking the young woman with you?'

'I don't see any reason why not. She's my assistant, and this pertains to a business matter.'

'Mr. Ellin is in the no-clothes section.'

'I still don't see any reason why not. Ms. Cowapoo, do you object to being seen naked by Bosley Ellin?'

'Oh, no. Certainly not. When in the no-clothes wing . . . '

The receptionist cleared her throat. 'Tub eighteen has been reserved for you, compliments of Mr. Ellin. Mr. Ellin is in tub seventeen.'

'Do you suppose he could spring for two tubs?' I nodded toward Donna. I figured better Bosley than Boogie.

'I . . . ' She was being called upon to make a decision in the name of the mighty Bosley Ellin. She blinked. 'Of course. How about tub sixteen for your assistant? Will that do?' She handed us each a key on a large wooden tag. 'You'll need these for your lockers.' To Donna, she said, 'And your name would be?'

'Donna Cowapoo, spelled C-o-w-a-p-o-o. Woman Friday.'

'For Mr. Ellin's billing,' the receptionist added quickly.

On our way to the locker rooms, I peered into the dining room at the antique round-backed chairs and tables covered with checkered oilcloth. The tables had salt and pepper shakers in the shape of happy little deer that looked like Bambis or maybe Rudolphs.

The glistening white halls of custom-built tubs at the rear of the hotel were surely one of the wonders of Skamania County, being designed rather like the blinding interior of a giant chicken's foot and offering something for soakers of all ages and imaginations.

The entrance to the halls was where the imaginary chicken's heel would be. Toilets, showers, and lockers were located at chicken-foot central.

The white hall that was the straight-ahead toe emitted the piercing, nerve-twisting echo of high-pitched screaming and laughing; children were allowed, bathing costumes required.

The toe to the right was for those adult bathers who were self-conscious about the size, or lack of, or shape of breasts, butts, bellies, and genitalia, or bathers who had received imperfect advice from counselors of moral behavior. Here bathing suits were mandatory.

The toe to the left was for women and men who didn't mind showing it off and men and women who didn't object to seeing what it looked like.

The bare-ass wing was about a hundred and fifty feet long, with windows that ran nearly to the ceiling of its fifteen-foot-high walls. A row of magnificent white porcelain tubs with ornate balled feet flanked each side of a central aisle.

I stashed my gear in a locker, took a quick shower, and joined Donna in the hall of bare asses. I groaned audibly when I saw Donna naked for the first time and received a weary grunt in response. 'Do you suppose I should walk behind you to tub eighteen just to make sure nothing happens to you on the way? Ambush or something. In the cowboy movies it was called riding drag.'

'Oh, for Christ's sake, no.'

'Maybe later,' I said.

She gave me a look and raised one eyebrow.

Down the bare-ass wing we strode, naked as the proverbial jaybirds: the wild-haired p.i., license in hand, with the copper-skinned Donna Cowapoo at his side — one of the hottest-looking women you'd ever want to imagine. A woman like that ordinarily had better taste, or sense, than to hang out with a drinker of screw-top red and reader of Euell Gibbons.

Each tub had a curved curtain rod around it. By adjusting his tub's curtain, a soaker could have a private chat with his girlfriend, watch the scenery outside in private, or bullshit with someone in one of the adjoining tubs. This was a Sunday, and so the hall was full. Most of the bathers left their curtains open, but Bosley Ellin, in tub seventeen, chose to keep his drawn.

What was I supposed to do when I got to Bosley Ellin's tub? Knock on his curtain? No. Call over the top.

That's exactly what I did. 'Mr. Ellin?'

I heard the sloshing of water.

'Mr. Denson, I presume.' The curtain parted. Ellin looked up at me, then at Donna.

'My assistant, Ms. Cowapoo,' I said. I gave him my private investigator's license with a Denson and Prettybird card tucked inside.

22

Employment for Robots in Kobe

I opened the curtain to tub eighteen and stepped into the full tub.

'Shit,' I said and came right out again, mopping the sweat that all but spurted from my face. I liked to stand in a shower with hot water blasting against the back of my neck, but this was just too much. I didn't understand the pleasure in soaking in water that was too hot for comfort; I felt the same way about people who sat around roasting in the sun. No, no, no.

I forced myself back into the water — *wow-oh-whoa*.

'That's what I say,' Donna said from her tub.

From the tub in between, Ellin said, 'Not a hot-springs man, I take it, Mr. Denson.'

I said, 'Some people like anchovies and others can't stand 'em. Same with sitting in hot water, I suppose.'

Ellin was a jowly-faced, balding man with small, light gray eyes resting like eggs above fleshy pouches. He looked something like the actor Broderick Crawford, for reasons that escaped me. Perhaps it was the combination of his jowls and gravelly bass voice.

He gave me back my license, which I set on the floor. He kept the business card.

'This is Ms. Donna Cowapoo,' I said.

Ellin shook Donna's hand, then mine. 'You do have some assistant, Mr. Denson.' He addressed me, but his eyes reflected the chocolate-brown of Donna's nipples.

I said, 'She knows her birds.'

Donna beamed.

'My secretary didn't want me to talk to you, Mr. Denson. She was quite opposed. She didn't like the business about you claiming to represent animals — '

'Animal people. Which is why I brought Ms. Cowapoo in on the case.'

'Animal people. She thought you were a lunatic. She's very protective of me, and there have been some threats made. There was that woman found dead in the Lewis River. Maria worries that some Earth Firster will fly off his nut in defense of the spotted owl.'

'I can see why your secretary has to be careful.'

Ellin looked at my card again, then set it on the floor by one foot of his tub. 'Your card says John Denson and Willie Prettybird. Is Mr. Willie Prettybird an Indian too, Mr. Denson?' he said, glancing at Donna.

'He's a Cowlitz and, they say, a medicine man.'

He said, 'And a medicine man to boot! My heavens! And here my secretary thought you were working for the Audubon Society or the Sierra Club. I'm curious, Mr. Denson. Also I don't have anything to hide. Would you like to tell me about your client?'

'Clients. The animal people. They're quite shy, as I said.'

'Given to a concern for the environment.'

'Oh, yes, they're quite worried about

the environment. Wouldn't you say that, Donna?'

'Deeply concerned,' Donna said.

I said, 'They're at a loss to express themselves adequately and thought they ought to have a professional ask some questions for them, and so here I am.'

'I don't mind games, Mr. Denson. The animal people hired you to do what, exactly? If you don't mind my asking.'

'Oh, no, certainly not. No problem. A spotted owl was murdered.'

'The one in the papers a few weeks ago.'

'That's right. Somebody wrung its neck and threw it onto the highway outside Sixkiller to get flattened by log trucks headed for your mill. The animal people feel this is a clear-cut case of murder, and they want the killer.'

Ellin looked amazed. 'They want the 'murderer' of a spotted owl? My God, what must they think about duck hunters?'

Donna said, 'Ducks don't like duck hunters, Mr. Ellin, and they don't like ospreys either, but they consider hunters and sea hawks as two of the many predators they have to dodge every year in order to get out of those murderous arctic winters. This is a case of a docile, trusting owl sitting in someone's lap — then *zipppppp!*' She wrung the neck of an imaginary owl.

Ellin leaned back in his tub, not knowing what to say.

'As you can see, they're entirely different cases,' she said. 'No sportsman killed that owl. The killer looked that owl in the eye and then wrung its neck. You can understand why the animal people are upset.'

Ellin looked at me. 'You're looking for the murderer of an owl. Where else to start than the villainous Bosley Ellin? Owl murder suspect number one, eh, Mr. Denson?'

'Oh, heavens no. I've got all kinds of possibilities. But why not a timber baron?'

Ellin squeegeed hot water from his face. 'Timber baron, indeed! What you don't get when you listen to the professional spotted owl lovers is the full story, Mr. Denson. If this owl bullshit had affected the interests of Weyerhauser or Georgia-Pacific, then none of it would have gotten as far as it has — begging your pardon, Ms. Cowapoo. There are trees growing on privately owned land as well as trees growing on state land. On the surface you'd think there'd be trees enough to keep a lot of saws turning, but there aren't. Why is that, Mr. Denson? You're the detective.'

'The law says timber cut from federal land has to be milled in the United States, but if you cut a tree from private land, you can have it milled wherever you want.'

Ellin sighed. 'Yup. They replace mill workers in Sixkiller with robots in Kobe. It's the modern world, Mr. Denson. Have you ever looked at the action in the deep-water port at Longview? That place is built on the business of shipping logs from the Pacific Northwest to Japanese mills, and now Louisiana-Pacific is getting ready to have logs cut in northern California milled in Ensenada, Mexico.'

Mills like the one Bosley Ellin ran at Sixkiller were probably going the way of typewriter manufacturers and small farmers. If he couldn't come up with timber to cut, Ellin was going to have to help train his people to find work in new occupations.

'Mr. Denson, I bet you're thinking, well then, Bosley Ellin, why don't you compete with the Japanese and the Mexicans? To which I say, Mr. Denson, with just what capital? Hmm? Meanwhile, the Japanese have grabbed half of our logs, and if the spotted owl takes the rest, we're forced out of the milling business. You're talking three hundred jobs at my mill in Sixkiller. Can you really blame me for taking this to court?'

Neither Donna nor I said anything. Ellin and the mill owners like him were flanked by environmentalists on one side and the multinationals on the other, a hard sell in Congress. In Ellin's opinion, the fix was in, and he was probably right.

'This never has been timber barons versus the spotted owl, Mr. Denson. It's been the Skamania-Pacifics thrown to the owls, and business as usual for the great gray corporations and the slicko CEOs holed up in their glass towers. Can you name just one of those sons of bitches?' He shook a raised fist, water running from his elbow, then sank deeper into the tub, with the water nearly to his chin. 'At least people know who I am. I have a name, odious as it may be to the politically correct. The evil Boz stalks.'

'Genghis Ellis.'

'Folks aren't thrilled at sacrificing their jobs so spotted owls will have enough squirrels to eat, Mr. Denson. Now we get to watch the entertaining spectacle of Earth Firsters and owl worshippers pleading to Weyerhauser and Georgia-Pacific: 'Oh, please, please, would you generous and beneficent multinational corporations be good citizens and send those poor little guys a couple of rotten snags to mill so they'll knock off their obnoxious whining?'' Ellin shook his head bitterly. 'The brother of the sheriff of Skamania County, a professor who ran the owl count for the Audubon Society, actually got himself arrested with the Earth Firsters protesting the shipping of logs to Japan; he lashed himself to a loading crane.'

Donna said, 'See there, Mr. Ellin? They're not all bad guys.'

'The Earth Firsters aren't stupid, Ms. Cowapoo. Look. They know that if mill bankruptcies pull the unemployment rate to eight or ten percent in Oregon and Washington, you'll see the *Seattle Times* and the *Oregonian* publishing spotted owl recipes in their food sections.'

'Cook them little babies up,' I said. 'Fried spuds and barbecued spotted. Mmmmm.'

Ellin laughed. 'Hell, if the federal budget wasn't so haywire they'd have conned the taxpayers into making up the difference between our best price and whatever it is they're paying robots in Japan. A little subsidy to calm us down. If we had Scoop Jackson and Maggie back, or Wayne Morse in Oregon, maybe we would have gotten some help. Old Wayne would've laid it to the sons of bitches. Why we had to elect a bunch of pussies in neckties is beyond me, begging your pardon, Ms. Cowapoo.'

What Ellin was saying had given me the glimmerings of an idea. I said, 'You're not the only mill owner with timber rights in the Gifford Pinchot, are you, Mr. Ellin? Whenever there is a shortage of anything and people want it, prices go up. Isn't that the way the world works? You're under no obligation to cut them when you buy them. If there are only so many trees left and the market is growing, you don't have to have a Harvard MBA to figure out that trees are going to be worth real money sometime down the line.'

Ellin batted at the hot water in front of him and looked at me. He was wondering where I was headed. 'As a matter of fact yes, that's precisely how it works, Mr. Denson.'

'It's my bet the owl was murdered for profit — or because of hormones. Suppose I'm a timber speculator. I buy low and get myself some insurance against forest fires and wait it out. If I buy low enough and hold on to my timber, and if the courts say it's okay to go ahead and cut it, I stand to make real money. But if owl mania stops the cutting, I lose.

Is that how it works?'

'I'm a mill owner, not a speculator, Mr. Denson. I buy timber to cut, not as something to sit on until the price goes up. It's difficult for me to answer your questions when I still don't know who you represent or what you're after.'

I shook my head vigorously. 'I'm not dealing in riddles or puzzles here, Mr. Ellin, I assure you. I mean it literally. I'm here on behalf of the animal people, and I'm looking for the murderer of that owl.'

Ellin mopped his forehead with the back of his arm; I wasn't sure whether the perspiration was from the hot water or a sudden suspicion that he was dealing with a potentially dangerous lunatic.

'Have it your way, Mr. Denson. It's more fun talking about animal people anyway. I'm not the only one who holds cutting rights to tracts in Gifford Pinchot, but I'm the guy you read about in the newspapers because I have a mill to defend and because I publicly object to getting screwed by ball-less politicians.'

I held my hands up, water dripping.

'Mr. Ellin, I assure you, I'm only after the truth.'

'Then, Mr. Denson, I suggest you check with the Forest Service in Seattle to see who gets to cut trees in Gifford Pinchot once this legal mess clears. There's where you'll find your timber speculators. It's all a matter of public record. There's no secret to any of it.'

★ ★ ★

Donna Cowapoo and I rode in silence the first few miles of the trip back.

'What do you think about Bosley Ellin?' I asked then.

'I think he could have killed the owl if he had the opportunity and was in the mood. I also think he could have murdered Jenny MacIvar, but not because of the owl count. It would have to be something more basic or elemental.'

'Marijuana?'

'He's too straight to smoke pot, and he doesn't have any need to sell it.'

She was right, I thought. Ellin had

enough money; he didn't have to take risks like that.

The Harkenrider house was coming up on my right; the turnoff to Calamity was next. 'I was thinking, Donna, you know with that owl count scheduled to start on the North Fork tonight, it might be fun to take a hike up there after dark. We wouldn't scare the owls off, would we?'

She looked disappointed. 'I'd like to go with you, but I can't make it. I've got a date tonight.'

'Oh. I see.' I was disappointed. I stopped at the sign and turned left toward Calamity.

'A date with Willie,' she added quickly. 'Not one of those other kinds of dates.'

'Willie. I see. And the gang you were with at the parade? The guy I saw standing behind you at the parade?'

Donna said, 'Willie and him and a couple of others. I think you should still go up to the North Fork tonight. In fact, I recommend it very highly.'

23

A Laugher on the North Fork

The sky was clear and cold with scattered clouds that slid past a bright, ringed moon as I lit out up the Lucky Buck. When I got to the turnaround on the North Fork where Lois Angleton and Eric Starkey had finished their walk, I found four vehicles, including Starkey's pickup and something that looked like an RV but which, according to neat lettering on the side, was a mobile field laboratory of the U.S. Fish and Wildlife Service.

I didn't see Willie's beater, but there were plenty of places for him to hide it farther down the valley.

I glanced at my watch, eleven o'clock. I got out and wrapped a wool muffler around my neck. Did the moon give me enough light to see, or would I have to use my flashlight? I started buttoning my coat. I heard a muffled *ka-honk, ka-honk* from a flight of geese.

I stopped breathing.

Again: *ka-honk, ka-honk*.

They were flying north. *North?* This was October and colder than the proverbial balls of a brass monkey, going-south time, and these geese were going north.

I thought: no, no, no, my fine-feathered friends, the other way. You're headed for Canada. South, you want to go. Baja or someplace warm.

I looked at the sky, thinking maybe I could see the geese, but the moon was momentarily blocked by clouds, and the night plunged into darkness. *Ka-honk, ka-honk*. Still south to north. It was spooky.

The confused geese and the clouds were gone shortly, and I continued up the trail by moonlight. It wasn't much of a trail in the daytime, and trying to negotiate it at night was rough going.

After about twenty minutes I could see flashlights up ahead scanning the trees. I slowed. This was supposed to be an open and aboveboard counting of owls, but I didn't imagine the party wanted Boogie Dewlapp's private investigator blundering in uninvited.

Then I heard the yelping of a coyote.

Then, ahead of me, voices. There was an edge to one of the voices, a man's.

The coyote began yelping again — if it was in fact a coyote. I thought it was an odd sort of yelp, staying on one pitch rather than rising as a coyote's ordinarily would.

Flashlight beams scanned the tops of Douglas firs.

More voices. The lights were doused.

The curious monotone yelping was followed by what I assumed was the yipping and yelping of a guaranteed for-real coyote. This one quickly knocked off his yelps and went straight to a high-pitched, baying howl; the howl rose, wavering, to the moon and heavens beyond. Then the howling ceased, and the coyote returned to its yipping and yelping.

The monotone yelper was, for the moment, silent.

Up ahead, I heard more voices.

Ahead and somewhere to my left, the feral, catlike screaming of a mountain lion echoed across the narrow canyon. This was a genuinely spooky scream. What a night to count owls!

The big cat screamed again, a real blood-chiller.

Then silence.

Another piercing, angry scream echoed through the cold night air, a real hair-raiser. My heart fluttered momentarily, and my mouth turned dry.

I kept going up the trail, spooked but determined to get as close as I could to my own quarry.

Then came the call of an owl from the opposite side of the canyon:

Hoo . . . hoo-hoo-hoo . . . hooo.

I knew that one: the great horned owl.

The beams of flashlights scanned the tops of trees just ahead.

Hoo . . . hoo-hoo-hoo . . . hooo.

Somebody swore softly. A man. He was shushed softly. A woman.

They doused their flashlights.

Hoo . . . hoo-hoo-hoo . . . hooo.

More heated talk, getting closer. They

were coming my way. Were they calling it a night? Yes, they obviously were. But these were nocturnal birds. Wasn't it early to be quitting?

I could hear them talking, but it was hardly more than a murmur and I couldn't make sense of it. They were coming down the trail toward me.

I retreated toward my bus, stepping quickly but not daring to turn on my flashlight.

Was it the panther? Were they stopping because of the panther?

I was well ahead of the owl counters by the time I saw the vehicles parked in the turnaround, and once in my bus I had a few minutes before they would arrive. I sat and listened to the night sounds.

Somewhere out there in the blackness a maniacal, lunatic laugh, *ha-ha-ha-oo-oo-oo-oo, ha-ha-ha-oo-oo-oo-oo*, rose in weird, mocking, demented runs of, well, looniness, for that is what it was, a Pacific loon. There was, no doubt, a lake or pond farther up the canyon. The laughing echoed crazily in the cold air.

Well, so you want to count spotted owls, do you? The loon thought that was just hysterical. *Ha-ha-ha-oo-oo-oo-oo*.

You want to stay out there in the cold with a restless mountain lion out there prowling around?

Ha-ha-ha-oo-oo-oo-oo!

Nuts, is what the loon thought of the party of bird counters, brandishing their university degrees and government titles. He possibly had a point.

Ha-ha-ha-oo-oo-oo-oo!

Did I know that loon? Could it be Donna or Willie? I thought: Willie Prettybird, you crazy, wild-ass son of a bitch, wonderful; if that's you, do it again!

The loon treated the fleeing ornithologists with a peal of laughter that was so demented and mocking it was downright spooky. *Ha-ha-ha-oo-oo-oo! Ha-ha-ha-oo-oo-oo! Ha-ha-ha-oo-oo-oo!*

The coyote began baying again. *Ow-wow-wow-woooooo! Ow-wow-wow-woooooo!*

The panther screamed.

Ha-ha-ha-oo-oo-oo!

I cranked up the bus and headed for Calamity before any of the counters spotted me.

24

When the Bean Dip Runs Out

By the time I got back to the Kokanee Vacation Cottages, the moisture in the air had begun to freeze, and the frost sparkled like crushed zircons on the oil-soaked gravel of the parking lot. I breathed great soft bursts of vapor as I walked quickly from my microbus.

The cabin was murderously cold. I turned up the thermostat on the ineffectual baseboard heater and leaped about on the icy linoleum flinging clothes this way and that. Finally, I dove, shuddering, into the musty bed.

I lay there warming my spot, thinking about the Harkenriders' story of Jenny MacIvar and Lois Angleton going in and out of both North and South Forks preparing for the owl count. *I know what she saw*. Jenny MacIvar had seen something on one of those trips.

259

What had she seen? Something at the caved-in shack on the North Fork of Jumpoff Joe? Something having to do with the pot found on the Harkenrider place on the South Fork? It was hard to believe anybody would shoot her over some weed. What about the threat mail she and Lois Angleton had received? Did it have something to do with the accuracy of the owl count? Possibly, but I had a feeling the reason for her murder was deeper and more basic than that.

I had no sooner gone to sleep than I was awakened by a slamming door and voices, then raucous laughter that all but burst the thin and rotting walls of my cabin. I heard Willie's voice, then Donna's, then the crunching of feet on newly frozen, crisp frost, then another burst of laughter. I slipped out of bed and used the heel of my hand to clear a spot on the moisture that had accumulated on the inside of the window.

I peered out; Willie Prettybird and Donna and four Indian males, including the one I had seen at the parade with Donna, were unloading beer and sacks of goodies from Willie's beater and Donna's old pickup. They looked ready to celebrate.

Willie had a half case of beer under each arm. 'Denson!' he called.

I quickly slipped on a pair of shorts and was at the door in two strides, holding it open so they could hustle their beer and groceries inside. No North Fork loon joined in their laughter and merriment, but this group had guilty-as-hell written large on their triumphant faces.

'Crap it's cold out there,' Donna said.

Willie ripped the tops off the cardboard boxes of beer and began stuffing the cans into the refrigerator. 'Well, by God, everybody, we woke up the Lone Ranger. Sleeping on the complexities of murder, Denson?'

'Helluva Tonto you are,' I said.

Willie gave me a hug. 'What would you do without me, Kemosabe? Your noble redman sidekick.'

'I'd have a whole lot less grief is what I'd have.'

Donna retrieved bags of Fritos and potato chips and bean dip from a paper sack, and assembled them on the counter of my tiny kitchenette.

'You folks been having a little fun on the North Fork tonight?' I started the business of introductions. 'John Denson.'

The first Indian, who was in his early forties with a bulging belly and a black-and-red checked shirt, extended his hand and said, 'Melvin.' Melvin peered over his nose at Willie and added, 'I'd think Prettybird'd have to be somewhere near the bottom of the Watson barrel.'

'A man does his best with the cards he's dealt,' I said. 'It's not always easy, I can tell you that.'

'Oh, for Christ's sake,' Willie said.

Duke, in his mid-thirties, wore a huge silver belt buckle studded with turquoise and a high-crowned cowboy hat that rarely left his head. He gripped my hand tightly, with much sympathy and pseudo-gravity, as befit the razzing of Willie Prettybird. 'You poor son of a bitch,' he said solemnly.

Toro, a broad-chested man in his early fifties, sported earrings and a pigtail. 'You can see how even we get a little tired of his noble-redskin shit.'

Little Eagle Brown, in his late twenties, wore suspenders, a checkered shirt similar to Melvin's, and an off-green Reggie's Café, Westport, Washington, baseball cap. It was Little Eagle that I'd seen standing behind Donna at the parade. He said, 'Shit, Willie!'

That said it all. It was the intonation more than anything else. Final stop.

I put the card table toward the edge of the sag so the floor wouldn't cave in under our weight, and in minutes the warped top was a litter of Olympia stubbies, cigarette butts, and small change.

I knew I shouldn't ask any one of them if he or she was a specific animal, Goose or Bear or whatever. Willie's friends never asked him if he was Coyote, and I had been told that the question pissed him off most royally.

I looked at Donna. 'Were all of you at the parade yesterday too?'

'The whole gang,' she said.

Willie grinned and took a slug of

Olympia. 'What'd you think? Is there any chance Kenny O'Callahan's owl is the same one the women from the Wildlife Service said got its neck wrung?'

'I'd say there was a chance of it. Anything's possible.'

Willie gave that some thought, then ripped the lid from an Oly and handed it to me. 'I hear you and Donna had quite a good time soaking it up with the Boz today. You know, Denson, Donna is one of us and we tend to feel protective toward her. You know how it is.' He arched one eyebrow and cocked his head to one side.

I shook my head in mock sorrow at his obvious stupidity. 'The deal is, Prettybird, if that's what your name really is, Prettybird . . . '

His friends all joined in with all manner of bird chirruping and jabbering — an entire flock of pretty birds. I was surrounded by wrens and finches.

' . . . your imagination immediately turns to bullshit as usual.'

'You mind telling us how you managed to wangle that session with Ellin?'

The birdmen ceased; they too wanted to know.

'I just drove on over to the mill there at Sixkiller and told his secretary that I was a private detective hired by the animal people to investigate the murder of a spotted owl on the highway. No problem.'

'Up-front's the best way,' Donna said.

Melvin's belly bounced with laughter; Cowboy Duke whacked his Stetson against his thigh; Toro, laughing crazily, held his pigtail straight out from his head; and Little Eagle Brown responded with an odd *hee-yuk, hee-yuk, hee-yuk* that was lifted straight from Goofy in the comics.

I said, 'I was out on the North Fork yesterday afternoon on my paying case. I heard some owls up there. I'd lay money that they were spotted owls.'

Willie glanced at his friends. Guilty as hell.

I said, 'On my way back to my bus, who should I find but Jenny MacIvar's boss skipping hand in hand with an Audubon Society professor from the University of Washington.'

'The sheriff's little brother.'

'And do you know something else, Willie? I saw your Dart chase after them toward Calamity.'

Willie looked chagrined. 'Have some bean dip, Denson. Clean out your valves. A tub of bean dip and a case of Olympia at the ready, that's the good life. There's a twenty-four-hour Mini-Mart down the road.'

'When the bean dip runs out, the good life comes to an end,' I said.

Willie shook his head. 'When the bean dip runs out, we run down to the Mini-Mart for some more. So you decided to take Donna's advice and drive out to the North Fork again tonight, eh, Denson?'

'When I got out of my bus the geese were flying north, and then I hiked up the trail into the canyon, and I heard a coyote.'

'A coyote?' said Willie, mock-astonished.

'Yes, I did, and a mountain lion and a great horned owl and finally even a loon.' There were repressed grins around the table. 'That wasn't you assholes out there, was it?'

They exploded with laughter, slapping the table triumphantly.

'That's what I figured. You're not going to do that every night, are you? Screaming panthers and maniac loons. Somebody murdered one of their owl counters, remember. They'll bring paratroopers down from Fort Lewis to jump your hides.'

'C'mon, white man. One night of fun is not going to hurt anything. Even bird freaks gotta laugh sometime. Where's their sense of humor?'

Little Eagle Brown said, 'We want them to know we're out there watching them.'

At two A.M. we came to the end of our capacity for celebration. Sodden with alcohol and exhausted from laughter, we settled down amid our party litter for what remained of the night; Willie and his pals had brought sleeping bags and lay at odd angles about the sagging floor.

Donna Cowapoo was snuggled into the cocoon of her sleeping bag on the fold-out bed.

I found it difficult to keep my eyes off her face. I just had to go and say, 'Good night, Donna.' Of course it was more than dumb of me to single Donna out for a good-night; it amounted to an open invitation for Willie and his pals to have a little fun.

Donna understood that. Her smile was wonderful through the dim light.

Willie and his pals waited for her reply.

'Good night, John.'

That triggered much merriment indeed. They nearly lost their wits with laughter. Good night, John. Ho, ho, ho!

'Oh, John, John!' Willie called.

'Donna!' Melvin sighed heavily.

'John, John!' Willie was very passionate now.

'Donna, Donna!' Melvin was beside himself.

I said, 'Oh, shut the fuck up, Willie.'

Willie pretended to be hurt. 'Did you hear him, Donna? Don't let that awful white man talk to me that way. Make him take that back!'

Donna didn't say anything. She didn't care what they thought or said.

After the last of the giggling and jokes had subsided, Willie said, 'By the way,

Denson, we've gotta be up and out of here in a couple of hours. These assholes have to go to work down in Oregon in a few hours.'

'Monday morning, Denson,' Melvin said. 'We can't lay around in the fart sack all day like you and Willie.'

That night I tossed and turned in bed and dreamed a long, surreal sequence of axes and chain saws and trees and birds and talons and women.

The dream opened with axes coming at me from all directions. The axes hit wood. Chips flew directly at my face. Chain saws replaced the axes; they too were everywhere, buzzing madly, rooster tails of sawdust looping from the cutting blades.

And then came the crashing of trees that I had to dodge, scrambling through underbrush as they came zooming down, each one headed straight for me, shaking my nightmare world like dice in a cosmic fist. And then the birds — hooting and screaming and floating in the air all around me.

A hawk folded its wings and plummeted in my direction.

Pursued by axes and chain saws and falling trees and screaming birds, I ran, holding my hands in front of me to protect myself from the underbrush.

I came to a great calm lake on a still day. On the lake, a naked woman floated on her back. Her eyes were closed. Her hair drifted lazily in the water. I reached out to grab her, but my arms were too short. I tried and tried, but it was no use.

I realized I was being watched.

From the gloom of a great dark forest, a second woman looked out at me with understanding eyes. I saw her face and her black hair, but the rest of her blended into the forest.

I stepped in her direction but she vanished in a heartbeat.

I turned, and the lake and floating woman were gone also.

By the time I woke up, sweating under my cocoon of blankets, Willie and Donna had departed with their friends. I'd never heard them leave.

25

As His Oats Grow Cold

I made myself a cup of coffee and put some oats on to boil. These weren't sissy rolled oats, but rather he-man smashed chunks of grain that required thirty minutes of honest boiling in salted water, and were worth every second of the wait because of the jaw-satisfying crunch of cooked cereal that resulted.

I saw through the kitchen window that a warm front had pushed through from the coast in the night: the frost of the previous few mornings had been replaced by a light drizzle. As I sat there crunching horselike on my oats, molars saying 'Go for it, John,' somebody knocked at my door, and a man's voice called, 'Denson!'

I pulled a pair of jeans over my shorts and opened the door: Sheriff Bert T. Starkey.

'Won't you come in, Sheriff?' I said,

grabbing for a shirt. The sheriff followed me inside. 'Pull up a chair,' I said over my shoulder. I cleared places in the party litter at the card table so we could sit down and, without asking if he wanted any, poured him a cup of coffee, which he accepted with a nod of thanks.

I sat down with a cup of my own, pushing aside dirty glasses, beer bottles, and wadded-up Frito and potato chip packages.

Starkey considered the clutter. 'Been doing a little partying, have you, Mr. Denson?'

'I had a few friends over last night. This visit has to do with what, Sheriff?'

Starkey was all business for it being so early in the morning. 'Mr. Denson, the business card you gave me the other day has John Denson and Willie Prettybird written on it. Is this Prettybird by any chance the Indian that has been seen coming in and out of your cabin here?'

'The same.'

'I see. Did he help you consume all this stuff?'

'Yes, he did. He and a few friends.'

'Is he involved in your investigation of the marijuana found on the Harkenrider place?'

'No, he isn't.'

The sheriff took a sip of coffee. 'Well then, why is he here? And where are these friends of his?'

'Boogie Dewlapp rented this cabin as a base for my investigation, and when Willie found out, he decided to crash here and maybe do a little fishing and have a good time.'

'Fishing?'

'That's right.'

'Do you know his whereabouts?'

'I don't have any idea. His friends had to go to work down in Oregon so they all took off early this morning.'

'How early this morning?'

'We threw it in at two o'clock. I damned near passed out when I hit the sack, and the truth is I don't know when they left. I was asleep.'

'Prettybird doesn't have to go to work, does he?'

'Willie scores a job here and there. But he's not a nine-to-fiver; he's not a wage slave if that's what you mean. He might have gone to have breakfast with them, or maybe he went to Oregon too. He's got an apartment in northwest Portland.'

The sheriff sighed. 'Mr. Denson, I have a good idea that you're not telling me everything you know here.'

'I'm telling you God's truth, Sheriff. Haul out the polygraph if you want.'

'Just who were these friends of his? Will you give me their names? He took out a pad and readied a ballpoint pen.

'Well, there was Melvin and there was Duke, and Toro, and Little Eagle Brown. Uh, and one woman, Donna.'

He finished scribbling. 'And Donna.'

Behind the sheriff's shoulder I saw Willie Prettybird's Dart pass by on the highway with two figures in the front seat. Willie and Donna had, in fact, been to breakfast. They had also seen the sheriff's car and would hang out somewhere until he was gone.

'And their last names?'

I said, 'Donna Cowapoo. Little Eagle Brown. I don't know the others.'

'They didn't mention any horsing

around on the North Fork last night, did they? Redskin frolics.'

'No, they didn't.'

'When were they here, Mr. Denson? Between what hours? You say you went to bed at two.'

'Let's see, I had a beer at the Hog Wild and got back about eleven-thirty or so, and they came in not long after that.'

The sheriff sighed. 'Now let me tell you a couple of things here, Mr. Denson. First, the people counting those owls are doing it against our advice. We haven't ruled out the possibility that whoever murdered Jenny MacIvar might be after Dr. Angleton as well. Second, Dr. Angleton believes somebody was up on the North Fork last night making like coyotes and panthers. Under the circumstances, like it or not, she and her party had to knock off early. They were not amused.'

'By the way, how is the murder investigation going?'

Starkey narrowed his eyes. 'A murder is police business, Mr. Denson, not yours. When we have something to make public, we'll tell it to the media, not some hotshot private detective.'

'Maybe there were coyotes and panthers up there. This is the great Northwest.'

'Loons, geese, great horned owls. Sure there were. One thing is sure: Sometime early this morning, somebody broke into the Hog Wild Saloon and stole that flattened owl they had hanging from the ceiling.'

'What?'

'If Willie Prettybird did break into the Hog Wild and steal that owl, he better be praying to the Great Spirit that I get to him before Kenny O'Callahan and his friends. Second, if I find out you've been lying to me about any of this, I'll have your boxtops.'

'I gave you the straight skinny, Sheriff.'

Sheriff Starkey got up and put away his pad and ballpoint pen.

I watched him walk through the mud back to his squad car. He opened the car door and kicked some goo off his fancy cleated walking shoes, but paused before he got in. 'By the way, you haven't found anything substantial in that Harkenrider case, have you? I hate to see kids like that take a marijuana tumble if they didn't have anything to do with the damned stuff.'

A sheriff with a conscience! This wasn't the Starkey I'd talked to in Minnie's. A man with murder on his hands and he's worrying about a pot case. 'I haven't found a thing, Sheriff, and that's a fact. I'm convinced they're innocent, but it beats hell out of me where the plants came from.'

'You know, Mr. Denson, it's my opinion that maybe seventy percent of what you're saying has any basis in fact, and the rest is plain, unadulterated horseshit.' He shut the door and drove off.

I went inside and found that after all the sheriff's palavering, my oats had grown cold. I poured myself another cup of coffee and meditated over the cold oats. Hot, they were delicious. Cold, well . . .

Why would Starkey have his mind on the Harkenrider pot?

In their quarrel on the North Fork, Eric Starkey had told Lois Angleton that 'he' would take care of them. 'He' would see that it was done.

Who was 'he'? Bert Starkey?

Who was 'them'? Terry and Mary Ellen Harkenrider?

Take care of what? Of seeing to it that Terry and Mary Ellen Harkenrider didn't take a rap for something they didn't do?

I abandoned my oats and fished the rubber tire prints and footprints out of my knapsack. I opened the front door, and damned if right there in the mud in front of me was a perfect match for the shoes that had made several trips in and out of the shack on the North Fork.

I kneeled, footprint mold in hand. Same shoes. No question. Bert Starkey, or some phantom wearing his boots, had delivered the Harkenrider marijuana in his brother Eric's van. But the sheriff could claim, with impeccable logic, that he'd left the footprints in the process of investigating outbuildings in the area after the bust at the Harkenrider place.

The phone rang.

'Dumbshit?' said Willie on the other end.

'The sheriff's gone,' I said. 'He thinks you stole the flattened owl from the Hog Wild early this morning. Did you?'

'We did our damnedest. It's a long story.'

'But you didn't lift it.'

'Well, yes and no.'

'What does that mean? Yes and no.'

'Your question was: did we steal it from the Hog Wild. The answer to that is truthfully no, but we do have it.'

'In your possession?'

'We got it.'

'Mmm. The sheriff might be hanging around looking for you still. I've got a couple of things I want to check out this morning; do you suppose you and Donna could come back this afternoon and bring the owl with you? Starkey will get bored waiting for you to show up here.'

'Done. Thank you, Chief.'

'Meanwhile, stash it someplace. Don't drive around with it in your car. Say hello to Donna.'

Donna, who'd apparently been listening in on the conversation, said, 'Hello, John. See you this afternoon.'

To some private investigators, I suppose, working for someone like Boogie Dewlapp carried with it the stigma of borderline sleaze, but the ol' Boog had his good points as well as bad.

If the Wesley Spooners that Boogie hired weren't the best or most experienced lawyers, he had worked out a cost-efficient system that had its advantages. The Dewlapp brothers had regular investigators in Seattle, Tacoma, Spokane, and Portland. Those detectives ran surveillances, shot pictures, and did other gumshoe duties; flunkies worked the phones for record checks and time-consuming bureaucratic inquiries.

It was a Monday morning and Boogie's secretary was always prompt in starting a new week. I called her and told her I needed a few details taken care of in the Terry and Mary Ellen Harkenrider case down in Sixkiller.

'Yes, sir, Mr. Denson, what can we do for you?'

This what-can-we-do-for-you offer could

be fairly translated as: If there's any way Boogie Dewlapp can save a dime in expenses just let us know.

I said, 'Well, thank you. I do have one little chore that I need taken care of. I'd like someone to check the records of the U.S. Forest Service to see who owns the timber-cutting rights in the Gifford Pinchot National Forest. I'm especially interested in the area around Sixkiller.'

'Gifford Pinchot National Forest near Sixkiller. Got it, Mr. Denson.'

'If you could get right on it, I'd appreciate it a whole lot.'

'You'll call us back this afternoon?'

'Will do.'

'Is that all, Mr. Denson?'

'That's enough for now, I think. Thank you very much.' I figured if Boogie ever questioned my request for info on rights to the timber in Gifford Pinchot, I'd tell him to bill the animal people.

26

How the Skimmers Got Switched

I followed the call to Boogie's office with one to the Vancouver district office of the Washington State Division of Highway Maintenance. After being put on hold, I lucked out and drew a woman whose tone of voice said she genuinely wanted to be helpful. It was a Monday morning; why not start the week out right.

I said, 'My name is Dr. Neil Irwin. I'm a visiting professor at the WSU extension here in Vancouver.'

'The agriculture extension?'

'That's correct. I'm studying the feeding habits of opossums, which are nocturnal. That's why you see so many of them at night, and why so many of them get run over. If it's possible, I'd like to talk to the maintenance worker who is responsible for keeping the highways clean in the Sixkiller area.'

She laughed. 'Let the highway workers find your possums for you, eh?'

'We haven't found a better way. When a bunch of them get squished on the highway, it means they're roaming around in the adjoining fields.'

'You would want to talk to Wayne Kerr or Albert Kunzman. I can leave a note for them to call you if you want, or you'll find them fixing busted pipes in the toilets at Ballyhoo Creek State Park. They'll be closing the place down the end of the month.'

'And where is that?'

'It's on the Lewis River about five miles east of Calamity. They should be out there until almost quitting time.'

Such a deal. That was just a few miles up the road from the Kokanee Vacation Cottages. 'Well, thank you,' I said.

'Good luck with the possums.'

I got in the bus and headed up the road along the Lewis to Ballyhoo Creek State Park, which was on the inside of a large curve in the river. The park had the usual picnic tables and benches in addition to toilets, as well as a softball diamond. Two state-licensed vans sat outside the toilets.

The moment I turned off my Volkswagen, I could hear swearing and metal banging on metal in the women's toilet. When I got close to the open door, I could hear a man say, 'Jesus, Wayne, did you ever see a woman with such bazooms in your life? I mean have you? They just stick right out there.'

'Incredible. Just incredible,' Wayne said.

'And her sister ain't bad either, in case you hadn't noticed.'

'You know something, Al, I'm tired of fucking with this thing. I don't give a damn if the taxpayers have to spring for a few extra bucks. Give me that goddamn hacksaw!'

'Atta boy,' Al said. 'It's time we had plastic stuff in here anyway. When was this put in here, thirty or thirty-five years ago? We'll be doing the taxpayers a favor.'

I stepped inside as the voices continued in one of the stalls.

Wayne said, 'This is gonna do it. Just cut this sucker right in half and get on with it. They're not paying me enough for me to contort myself back there with my face on this floor. No fucking way. Grab that for me, will you, Al?'

I stopped in front of the open door of the toilet to see Wayne, rump stuck up, struggling with a hacksaw behind the toilet. All was bent over holding something with his right hand.

'Hello in there,' I said.

They turned, grateful for any reason for a break.

'My name is Trevor Henley and I'm with the Federal Bureau of Investigation. I'm here as part of the investigation into the death of Jenny MacIvar of the Fish and Wildlife Service.' I flopped my private investigator's ID in front of them and flipped it closed before they had a chance to read it.

'The lady in the papers, eh?' said the man with the hacksaw. 'Name's Wayne. This's Al.'

'Right. The woman who was killed and her friend came to see you a while back about a spotted owl that had been found flattened between Sixkiller and Calamity.'

Wayne and Al exchanged a quick

glance. It was meant to be covert, but was not.

This was pay dirt of some kind. I said quickly, 'You have to understand, I'm not interested in the owl itself. I don't care what happened to the carcass, except that Dr. MacIvar later said there was a flattened great horned owl as well as a flattened spotted. She said she and her supervisor drove off with the great horned owl that'd been destroyed by a shotgun blast and left the spotted behind. We have to check out all details and possibilities on something like this.'

'Oh, yeah, I can see where you'd have to do that,' Wayne said.

'All I want to know is how that mistake came to happen. Is it possible that those women inadvertently just drove off with the wrong bird? Was that it, an accident? If something else happened, I want to know.'

Wayne laughed. 'What do you say, Al?'

Al grinned. 'Tell him.'

'Last spring me and Al here were playing darts up at the Hog Wild Saloon, and we were laughing about floppers and

286

skimmers and stuff when this guy says he'd pay us two hundred bucks for a dead spotted.'

'Floppers and skimmers?'

Wayne laughed. 'A flopper's an animal that's just been killed, and you got broken bones and blood and guts and stuff to clean up. A flopper can get ripe fast on a hot summer day. Whew! A skimmer's one that's been run over so much it's been flattened and all the juices squished out and dried up, and so they're an easier deal. You just sort of skim them up off the highway with a shovel.'

'Hence the name. Go on, tell me what happened.'

'Well, Al and me came across this skimmer that was clearly a spotted owl. We'd been reading about them in the papers and everything, and we had a good idea what one looked like. We wanted to score the two hundred bucks with the guy at the Hog Wild, but just to cover ourselves decided to report it also. It was all Al's idea, though; I didn't have anything to do with it.'

Al said, 'Fuck you too, you asshole.

Hey, no way did we think they'd want to cart a skimmer off. Right, Wayne? Who in the hell'd want a dried-up skimmer? A juicy flopper, we could see maybe.'

'A skimmer, can you imagine?' Wayne said. 'That bird had taken a real pounding on the highway. *Ka-whack, ka-whack, ka-whack* all day from log trucks headed for the mill at Sixkiller. It was more like a piece of cardboard with feathers than anything else.'

'Well, what happened exactly? Can you tell me from the beginning?'

Wayne said, 'What happened was that the two woman . . . '

'Ornithologists.'

'Right. After all the palaver and them thanking us for calling them and everything, the women threw our spotted skimmer into their rig and then went inside to the john. Me and old Al were pissed, but there wasn't much we could do.'

'Then the bald guy,' Al said. 'It wasn't us, honest.'

'Right. With the women in the john, the bald guy quick as a flash opened the back door of the van and grabbed the spotted and threw it in the garbage can where we'd tossed the great horned skimmer, and he fished out the great horned and put it in the back of the van. Ain't that what happened, Al?'

'That's it exactly. He hustled, man. It was obvious he didn't want them to catch him red-handed.'

'A bald guy? What bald guy is that?'

'They brought this bald guy with them, big dude,' Wayne said. 'He was real pleasant and all, but mostly didn't say anything. But I'll tell you one thing, bub, he sure as hell was quick when he got a chance to switch them owls. That sucker moved.'

'What can you remember about him? What did he look like? What was he wearing?'

Wayne said, 'He was a big guy, tall, and quiet. Women would probably say he was good-looking, wouldn't you say so, Al?'

'He didn't do anything for me.' Al grinned and took a step back from Wayne.

Wayne looked disgusted. 'Oh, shit, Al! He was a big, square-jawed guy, perfect features. I guess he just about had everything he could want except hair.'

I said, 'He wasn't some kind of photographer, was he?'

Wayne narrowed one eye. 'Right. Now that you mention it. He probably was a photographer.'

'Wore a vest with all this fancy gear,' Al said.

'Pockets everywhere,' Wayne added.

I turned as though I were ready to go, then stopped. 'By the way, you got to peddle your spotted skimmer, I assume.'

'Oh, yeah,' Wayne said.

'To what's-his-name, Kenny O'Callahan, president of the Committee for Loggers' Solidarity. Is that the guy you sold it to?'

Wayne laughed. 'I see you been having a beer at the Hog Wild.'

Al said, 'Did you see that list of who's going to show up for that auction? Jesus!'

'Closing in on thirty,' I said.

'All the way from southern Oregon.' Wayne was impressed. 'That skimmer's going to earn them loggers a few bucks, it's so.'

Al said, 'O'Callahan was thinking, you

have to give him credit.'

'That's okay, me and Al had fun down in Portland with our two Benjies, didn't we, Al?'

'We sure as hell did. Fried razor clams at Jake's.'

Wayne said, 'Why in the hell did the bald-headed guy switch them owls, if you don't mind me asking? It's not that Al or me said a word when the women got out of the john, mind you. We just sat there grinning like assholes and let them drive off with the wrong owl.'

I said, 'As I said, you two are in no trouble — good for you for scoring the two hundred.'

Wayne looked relieved. 'Whew! I was wondering.'

I gave him as grave and somber a face as I could muster. 'But you understand that the questions I asked are part of a government investigation. I'm sure you can appreciate the need for them to remain confidential.'

'Mum's the word,' Wayne said.

Which was total nonsense, of course. I could see that Wayne and Al couldn't wait to tell their friends about how an FBI agent investigating the murder of that woman scientist had asked them questions about the spotted owl they sold Kenny O'Callahan.

I left hoping they didn't hear me crank up that distinctive Volkswagen air-cooled engine. Not many FBI agents drive around in twenty-year-old Volkswagen buses, I don't imagine.

* * *

I drove back to my cabin to await the arrival of Willie and Donna and dialed Boogie Dewlapp's number in Seattle. Had Boogie's ever-scrounging flunkies had enough time to find out who owned rights to what timber in the Gifford Pinchot?

Boogie's secretary said yes, they had indeed completed the inquiry.

'What did you find?' I said.

She said, 'Most of the tracts were bought within the last three years by Bosley Ellin of Sixkiller, Washington, but some prime tracts were sold in 1982 when the market bottomed out during the recession. Those were bought by Avin Corporation, a Chicago commodities firm, operating on behalf of Elise Paxton Northlake, of Evanston, Illinois. She paid fifty dollars a thousand board feet.

'Mr. Dewlapp says owing to the shortage of logs, the Northlakes could now sell their timber for nearly twenty times that much — if they are allowed to cut it. He was curious and had me check out the Northlakes through our contact in Chicago. It turns out that Elise is the only child of Robert Paxton, the computer chips guy. You've probably heard about him.'

Yes, I had. Worth literally billions, according to the financial magazines. 'You said 'the Northlakes'?'

'She has a husband — a wildlife photographer, Mr. Denson. Is that of any help?'

'Plenty of help, thank you very much. And do tell Boogie, thank you. His bloodhound is closing in.'

I was indeed. Adonis Northlake's frequent 'fund-raising' trips East that had so annoyed Jenny were now explained. When Jenny MacIvar found out about Northlake's marriage, as she somehow must have, the man must have been furious. He could not afford for Elise to find out. Could not.

Here was the territory of murder.

27

An Owl Is What It Eats

Willie Prettybird was a cheery-looking redskin indeed as he peered through the carrot tops that stuck out of one of the two heavy bags of groceries he carried; although he stepped into a puddle and stumbled momentarily, he continued on with a triumphant bounce to his step.

No doubt about it, Willie was feeling good.

Behind him, Donna Cowapoo, with yet a third sack, looked equally buoyant.

Willie said, 'I figured with all this running around, we should treat ourselves to a good meal. See if Donna knows how to boil water.'

I went out to help Willie and made a grab for a carrot, but he sidestepped me with a sweet move. 'Stay out of there, dammit. We've got a use for those carrots.' He nodded cheerfully to his car.

'There's beer on the back seat.'

I collected the two half-cases of Henry Weinhard and hustled to catch up with Willie and Donna, who were putting away the groceries by the time I got inside.

'I take it Melvin and the gang will be coming back.' I started pouring water in my coffeepot.

'They may or may not,' Willie said. 'It doesn't make any difference. If we have meat left over, we'll have sandwiches tomorrow.' He started pitching tubers into the vegetable bin, his rump stuck up at me. 'I figured Donna could make us one of those pot roasts. You know what I mean, chief, one of those deals with carrots and potatoes and onions and turnips and stuff.'

'Just like his mommy used to make,' Donna said.

Willie abandoned the vegetable bin and started pawing through the cupboard. 'I saw there was a big pot in here with a lid on it. Where the hell'd that go?'

I poured us all cups of coffee while they got the food squared away and found what they needed to cook it in. 'Do you want to tell me about the owl?'

Willie grinned. 'They're making a big fuss about it on the radio. You'd have thought it was the Brinks heist.'

'Did you swipe it?'

'Like I said, the answer is yes and no, Denson. Little Eagle Brown and me and Duke and Toro and Melvin . . . '

'Me too,' Donna said.

'And Donna. All of us. We went out to the Hog Wild at about four o'clock, fully prepared to do whatever was necessary to steal that owl, I admit. But . . . ' Willie shook his head.

'What went wrong?' I asked with resignation; it almost always was the most profitable first question.

'Listen to what happens. We put Duke as a lookout on the road this side of Calamity, and we drop Melvin downstream, and Toro on the road to Sixkiller so we have everything covered, see. Then we park our car up the Lucky Buck so Toro can keep an eye on it, and Donna and Little Eagle Brown and I hike on down to the Hog Wild. We hide for a few minutes in the shadows to make sure everything is cool, and we're about ready to make our move when we get three hoots from Toro.'

'An '*oh shit! heads down!*' hooting, I take it.'

'You got it. In this case it's a car coming down the Lucky Buck. We stay put and watch while the car slows and turns around and comes back and pulls into the Hog Wild parking lot and stops. A bald guy gets out and puts on a pair of heavy leather gloves . . . '

Adonis Northlake!

' . . . He takes a look around and hops up on the porch, and without a pause or a glance over his shoulder, he smashes the window with his fist. He removes the pieces of glass with his gloves and steps inside.'

'What'd you do?'

'Little Eagle Brown and I scrunch down in the shadows of the porch, one on either side of the stairs. We look at one another and know it's now or never if we want to get that owl. Baldie comes out not a half minute later and bounds down the steps, owl in his right hand, which is on Little Eagle's side. Little Eagle's all balls, you have to give it to him, man, and he snags that mother and is gone, pow, sprinting for the shadows. You'd have thought he was Jerry Rice headed for the end zone.'

'Baldie doesn't have a chance, I take it.'

'Not a chance. He starts out after Little Eagle, but he pauses when he hears me take off behind him, and that's it. Little Eagle is gone. History. Jim Thorpe couldn't have beat him.' Willie reached into one of the paper grocery bags that was almost empty; he removed a clear plastic bag that had the owl in it rolled in a circle.

He spread it flat on the table. 'Here it is, man, the murder victim, cadaver courtesy of Little Eagle Brown. Not much to it except for feathers, but look there. You don't have to be a veterinarian to tell that its neck was wrung.'

I turned it over, saw that Willie was right, then got up and retrieved my notebook and the telephone book; watching Willie admire his score, I called the St. Helens Motel in Sixkiller and asked for Lois Angleton.

She was home.

'Dr. Angleton, I'm John Denson, the private investigator you met at Delbert's Awful Onion a couple of days ago. I hope you remember me.'

'Of course I remember you. What can I do for you, Mr. Denson?'

I said, 'I have come into possession of the flattened owl that they've been talking about on the radio.'

'The one stolen from the Hog Wild.'

'That's correct. I believe it may be the flattened owl you and Jenny MacIvar thought you had misplaced over at Sixkiller a few weeks ago. I was wondering if you might run an autopsy on it to see what we can learn from it.'

There was silence on the other end of the line.

'You and Jenny didn't misplace it,' I said. 'It's almost certainly the same owl Kenny O'Callahan showed off in the loggers' solidarity parade, and if my hunch is right, a proper examination of that owl may tell me who murdered Jenny.'

'I'd love to examine that owl, Mr. Denson.'

'Now? Today? In a couple of hours, say?'

'I have my lab parked out front, and it has everything I need to check that owl out. That's unit twelve. I'll stay put this afternoon.'

'Is this a complicated or time-consuming process, Dr. Angleton?'

'It should only take a few minutes for me to find out what I have to know — depending on how much is left of the bird.' I hung up.

Willie Prettybird started peeling a clove of garlic with a paring knife and the side of his thumb. 'What're you thinking, Kemosabe?'

'I'm not sure, Willie. Depending on what this woman finds in the owl, we may want to mount a war party pretty damn quickly. Do you suppose you could round up Little Eagle Brown and your pals for a little action tomorrow night?'

'Do I suppose? Could I?' Willie looked offended. He cut the peeled clove of garlic lengthwise and started rubbing it on the roast. 'Let's do it. Go see what the bird woman says.'

'Shouldn't take more than an hour or two.'

'Go then. Get that piece of shit of yours on the highway and rolling. Donna and I will get this roast going.'

'I'm on my way.' I headed for the door.

'When you come back we'll pig out, and I'll head to Portland for the war party.'

★   ★   ★

Lois Angleton's laboratory van looked like an austere RV on the outside, but the Fish and Wildlife Service had gone to considerable expense to give it one of those fascinating hightech interiors in which every hook and knob and indentation has more than one function.

In addition to doodads no doubt originating in research for the space program, the vehicle contained a darkroom, an examining table, a refrigerator and freezer, a toilet, a small kitchen, and drawers everywhere. No space went unused.

I sat down on a prosaic couch at the

end of the van and told her Wayne and Al's story while she spread the owl on the stainless-steel examining table and assembled her knives and pincers and microscope and other gear.

She looked incredulous. 'Adonis? Adonis Northlake switched those owls?'

'They said a good-looking bald man in a photographer's vest.'

'Why?'

'It's a long story, Dr. Angleton, and I'm not sure I have all of it figured out yet.'

'You said if I examined this owl it might help you find Jenny's murderer. You think Adonis Northlake murdered Jenny?'

I shrugged. 'I think a conviction is premature until I get all the facts.'

'But you think it's possible.'

'Anything's possible.'

She said, 'We did go to the john before we left, I remember now. Later we just couldn't believe we'd taken the wrong owl.' She unhooked a stool from the wall, unfolded it, sat on it, and considered the task before her.

I said, 'As I see it, there are two possibilities.'

'Possibilities for whoever it was who killed Jenny?'

'Right, two sets of motives . . . '

'Go ahead, Mr. Denson, it's okay if you talk while I work.' She flattened the bird on its back and stared at its dried-out torso.

'One motive might be made clear by your examination of this owl. You might be able to help me with the second as well, I'm not sure.'

She leaned over and examined the bird with a magnifying glass. 'I'm listening.'

'There is also a third possibility that would require questions about Jenny's personal life.'

She put the magnifying glass down. 'Jenny told me how you rescued her from the wind that night in the gorge, Mr. Denson.'

'The whole story or an expurgated version?'

'The whole story. She thought very highly of you, and under the circumstances, I'm sure she wouldn't mind my answering your questions.'

'I thought very highly of her as well, which is why I want to find her murderer. You know, Dr. Angleton, when I worked up the nerve to ask Jenny about the inevitable man, she went through an extraordinary listing of Adonis's many charms and merits. If he was that great, I wonder, just why did she allow herself to be charmed by a yahoo Galahad in a Volkswagen bus with a door that rattles?'

'I worked with Jenny for close to six years, Mr. Denson. Everybody thought she and Adonis were the perfect couple; I know I did. Jenny was full of energy and ideas, and Adonis was quiet and steady, the perfect man, to hear Jenny tell it. He could do no wrong.'

'But?'

'But then a couple of months ago she suddenly began to change. She still said Adonis was the perfect man, and she loved him and everything, but her attitude toward him was different. Jenny was hurting inside. From what, I don't know.'

'Did she tell you that Adonis had a wife in Chicago?'

Lois looked up from the owl. 'What? A wife? Adonis? No.' She shook her head. 'That can't be so.'

'Married to Elise Paxton, the daughter and sole offspring of Robert Paxton of microchip fame.'

'Adonis Northlake, married? Are you sure?'

'To the heiress of the Paxton microchip fortune.'

'Adonis? I can't believe it. He seemed so devoted to Jenny. He's caring and thoughtful and civilized and generous . . . He doesn't have a dishonest bone in his body. Not one. He — '

'Furthermore, he told the police he was engaged to Jenny.'

'Engaged to Jenny? I . . . Mr. Denson, I have to tell you, a man called me. Richard Chenoweth, he said he was. A jeweler at Gayle's in Portland. He said — '

'That Adonis had ordered a hot-damn engagement ring.'

She looked wide-eyed. 'I didn't believe him. I thought it was a crude joke. How do you know about that call?'

'That was me, Dr. Angleton, trying to find out if Jenny had told you about any engagement. Richard Chenoweth is an acquaintance of mine, an ophthalmologist in Portland.'

'Jenny didn't tell me anything of the sort. And she would have, I swear. Jenny and I were close friends as well as colleagues. We weren't at all competitive. We liked one another. If Adonis had asked Jenny to marry him, she would have told me.'

I believed her. I didn't say anything.

'She would have. Jenny found out about his wife, didn't she, Mr. Denson? Is that what happened? It's hard to believe that Adonis would lie about something like that, it truly is.'

'I think there's a strong possibility of it.'

'Do you think Adonis murdered Jenny?'

I shrugged. 'I think he had a reason, but I have to check out all the possibilities. Jenny said the first thing you do is search out the nests. I take it that means you do a lot of hiking in backcountry.'

'We can spot some nests with aerial photography, but mostly we have to get out there in the trees and take a look for ourselves. Those regurgitated fur balls pile up in the nest, and whenever we get a chance we bring them back to the van to analyze.'

'Got into pretty isolated areas, did you?'

'After the lawsuit we didn't want to miss any nests, so we made sure we looked everywhere. Our reputations were at stake. We didn't want Bosley Ellin's lawyers to make one single claim they could back up in court. Not one. Exactly what is it you're getting at, Mr. Denson?'

'When you scouted that area on the North Fork where you started your owl count, did Jenny ever say anything about seeing a man putting something in an abandoned shack up the trail? You know the one.'

Lois hesitated.

Quickly, I said, 'I was poking around the North Fork the day you and Eric Starkey quarreled about what Jenny had seen. I heard almost all of it, I think.'

'Ahh, I see. Your bus was there, I remember. The sleuth ever at work. Well, good. I was thinking of talking to you about it anyway. Jenny said she was hiking up the North Fork one afternoon and caught this guy red-handed putting marijuana plants in that shack. She just laughed and went on her way. She said she caught a glimpse of his face, and later she saw his picture in the paper. Or his double, almost. Jenny wasn't sure enough to complain to anybody.'

'Sheriff Starkey?'

'I told Eric about it. I said if that was his brother I didn't care how much pot he grew, but he couldn't put that young couple in jail for it. I told him that unless something was done, I'd have to talk to you about it. I knew you were working on the case from when I met you in that fast-food place in Calamity.'

'I don't think you have to worry about them going to jail.'

Lois Angleton looked relieved and turned her attention to the avian corpse. 'I don't know whether Jenny told you how this works, but what an owl does essentially is gobble its prey whole. A hawk does the same thing. An owl's stomach removes the meat and fluids, and the bird regurgitates a ball of fur and bones a couple of times a day.'

'About once every twelve hours, I think Jenny said.'

'That's right. When we trap a bird or get one that's been accidentally killed, we bring it back here and take a look at its fur ball.'

With a pair of tweezers, she carefully removed the tiny squashed lump and placed it on a glass slide. She slid the glass into a clip under the microscope lens and peered down at the pellet. She adjusted the microscope, and began pulling apart the pellet with her tweezers, carefully separating its layered contents.

She put down her tools, sat back, and pulled a book from the shelf, running her fingernail down the index. She turned to a page somewhere in the middle and read for a minute.

She looked into the microscope again, then back at the book. Then up at me. 'You say this is the same owl Jenny and I went out to examine by Sixkiller?'

'Unless those two guys were lying, and I don't think they were. They thought I was an FBI agent.'

She looked back at the lens again and returned to her meticulous chore of separating the parts of the pellet.

'They said they watched Adonis swap the owls while you and Jenny were in the women's room.'

'And you say their story was they sold it to this Kenny O'Callahan for two hundred dollars?' She adjusted the microscope.

'They didn't seem to have any doubt that it was the same owl O'Callahan had hanging in the Hog Wild. It's possible that he had two such owls, but I find that hard to believe.'

'For an owl found outside Sixkiller, this specimen is most unusual, I must say.' She looked up from the microscope, then back down.

'Why is that?' I got up and leaned over her shoulder, as though that would help me with my answer.

'Mr. Denson, I don't believe this owl

came from the Sixkiller area. It may have been found there, but it didn't come from there.'

'No?'

'It didn't come from the state of Washington, even.' She looked up again. 'I suppose it could be from the southwestern-most corner of Oregon.'

'What?'

'But northern California is most likely, judging from the moths it'd been eating. The pellet in its innards is mashed flat along with everything else, but I can still pretty well make things out. It lived in redwoods, Mr. Denson, not Douglas firs. Of course, if you turned it loose in a proper habitat here, it would do fine.'

'You're saying it was *brought* to Sixkiller?'

'I'd swear to it in court. These are not migratory birds, Mr. Denson. They may drift from area to area within their range, but they do not fly from northern California to southwest Washington, much less in the twelve hours necessary for this owl to still have this pellet in its innards.'

I thought a minute. 'Tell me, if this bird

had expelled this incriminating wad of gunk and you had captured it as part of your study, would you have had any reason to suspect it was from northern California, and not Gifford Pinchot?'

Lois Angleton closed her eyes momentarily and sighed. 'No, we would not, Mr. Denson. I see what you're getting at.'

'I recall Jenny telling me that you had done your best to make an accurate count the first time, and you believed in your work. She said there wasn't any logical reason for a dramatic surge in the owl population in Gifford Pinchot. Well, there you have one.'

'Somebody has been importing owls from northern California and releasing them here?'

'That's what I think.'

'Who?'

'Adonis Northlake. That's why he switched the owls.'

28

Rewards of Watching the Credits

Willie Prettybird, Donna Cowapoo, and I ate pot roast and drank screw-top red while we watched the local television news. The stealing of Kenny O'Callahan's spotted owl was given the dubious honor of being the day's regional lead.

Reporters and cameramen had been dispatched down from Seattle and up from Portland to videotape old farts and suspendered loggers sitting on barstools in the Hog Wild.

The story opened with a reminder of earlier charges of spotted owl murder on the road from Calamity, followed by a videotape of Kenny O'Callahan brandishing the owl in question at the parade in Sixkiller.

The broken window was shown. Then O'Callahan pointed at the ceiling where the owl had been hanging. O'Callahan, microphone thrust in front of him, charged that Earth Firsters were Private Property Lasters; he said they had committed common burglary. The guilty party ought to be locked in the big house over at Walla Walla and the key thrown away.

A female spokesperson for the Earth Firsters declined direct comment on the charge, saying of O'Callahan, 'My, he certainly is a big, brave fellow, isn't he? Does he know what hyperbole means?'

The pretty young reporter, a member of television's kiddie corps, was serious-faced as she delivered her summation from the steps of the Hog Wild. 'Skamania County Sheriff Bert Starkey says he has no clues as to the identity of Jenny MacIvar's murderer. Starkey declines to speculate if there is a connection between her death and the count of spotted owls that began last night in the Gifford Pinchot amid reports of howling coyotes and snarling panthers. Then, sometime early this morning, thieves broke into the historic Hog Wild Saloon here in Calamity and made away with the flattened spotted owl that was to have been auctioned in a loggers' benefit.

'As Starkey and his deputies continue their investigation, a couple of things seem certain: There are strange goings-on in this neck of the woods, and the town of Calamity, Washington, is living up to its name.'

With the news over, the pot roast a third gone, and a sated Willie Prettybird on his way to Portland to rustle up his irregulars, Donna Cowapoo and I drove to the aggrieved Hog Wild to see how the one-night celebrity regulars were bearing up under the fuss.

The story had been in the news all day, and judging from the number of Oregon license plates, carloads of the curious had taken spontaneous let's-do-it drives to Calamity to have a look at the fateful Hog Wild Saloon. The parking lot was full, so I parked my bus out on the road at the end of a line of vehicles.

Donna and I could hear the thump of bass and the whine of steel guitar before we stepped inside to the babble and hubbub. It was Monday night and on the television set above the bar, the San

Francisco Forty-niners battled the New York Giants. They did this soundlessly, as the jukebox played on. A deep-voiced man sang:

Well, I zip my jeans
And I boogie out the door,
My heart in my mouth,
Left woman number four.

Woman number four!
Woman number four!
I bet my brand new Ford,
There won't be any more.

Well, I bought that Ford
On the easy payment plan.
Drove it off the lot,
Said I'll pay you when I can.

Woman number four!
Woman number four!
I bet my brand new Ford,
There won't be any more.

Donna and I eased through the crowd and joined several beer drinkers who had collected around the bulletin board. A solidarity committee proclamation, signed by the furious O'Callahan himself, placed a one-thousand-dollar bounty on information leading to the return of the owl and the arrest of the thief 'on charges of felony breaking and entering into the Hog Wild Saloon in Calamity, Washington, and for grand theft, spotted owl carcass.'

O'Callahan used the word 'bounty,' which I thought had an untoward KKK ring to it, suggesting posses and vengeance, rather than the more neutral 'reward,' which offered courts and the hope, if not prospect, of justice.

And what was the point of fame if not to enjoy? Kenny O'Callahan was at the dart board with his buddies, which was probably where he was every Monday night. Between turns the players bullshitted with their buddies and listened to the jukebox while they watched the soundless clash of armored combatants.

I led Donna through the crowd to the bar and ordered us each a bottle of Henry Weinhard. We found a place to stand within eavesdropping distance of the dart companions: O'Callahan and Ron and Charlie with the Caterpillar baseball cap.

Ron said, 'She sure as hell fried your ass, bub.'

'Bitch,' O'Callahan said.

'That word 'hyperbole' means gross, outlandish exaggeration, in case you haven't looked it up.'

'Fuck you and the horse you rode in on.'

'You have to remember to keep your cool next time. You give a bitch like that an opening, and she'll slam you one good. Oh, you big, brave fellow, you.' Ron made a kissing sound and let his hand go limp.

O'Callahan, looking for relief, spotted me through the crowd. 'Hey, Mr. Detective dart thrower.'

I escorted Donna to the board, watching O'Callahan eyeing her as we picked our way through the bodies.

O'Callahan said, 'Did you see the bounty we posted for the son of a bitch who stole our owl? Maybe someone like you could run the mother down. Put a professional on the case.'

'It's a case of burglary, isn't it? I

assume Sheriff Starkey is looking into it.'

O'Callahan laughed bitterly. 'That pompous fuck-off! All he wants to do is drive around looking at that picture of himself on billboards. It's enough to make a grown man puke.'

'I don't have any objection to picking up a few spare bucks for delivering a thief on the side. One of the perks of being an independent.'

'If you can deliver the mother who stole our owl, you'll get your money.'

'Of course, I'll keep an eye peeled.'

'You want to throw a few?'

'Naw,' I said. 'I believe I'll go home early and get a little sleep tonight.'

'A little sleep, sure,' he said, watching Donna out of the corner of his eye.

Donna and I did go back early, but we didn't go right to sleep or try to grope one another. Instead we retreated to our respective nests and flipped through the channels to check out the various versions of what was happening in Calamity, and blundered into the beginning of a documentary on raptors — that is, hawks, eagles, and owls.

This was part of a new series of nature documentaries on public television narrated by the grave, civilized voice of the actor Charlton Heston.

We watched a red-tailed hawk nail a blackbird midflight. We followed an osprey as it dove into the water and rose with a wriggling fish in its beak. And, courtesy of an infrared camera, we even got a spooky shot of a spotted owl flying softly among mammoth trees in the black of night.

During the flight of the seldom-seen spotted owl, Charlton Heston told us how owls had extra large wings with specially evolved feathers that enabled them to stay aloft with fewer beats of their wings than other birds. This ability to fly extra slowly, nearly hovering at times, allowed owls to spot their quarry at night and pick their way through trees in a crowded forest.

Next came a daylight shot of a spotted owl nest, this one built in the broken top of a big cedar in the state of Washington. The cedar, said Heston, was more than four hundred years old.

Heston said environmentalists believed

that this northern species of the spotted owl was endangered because of the 'degradation of its habitat.' I admired the grave manner in which the sonorous Heston intoned two-bit words like 'degradation' and 'habitat.' The lower the voice and the more gravelly the delivery, the greater the authority, and nobody, but nobody, challenged Charlton Heston.

The nest was followed by a shot of a big cedar crashing to the ground. The camera showed a ridge denuded by clear-cutting and the rapacious new resident that had moved in: the great horned owl, shown diving for a groundhog that had been so foolish as to go topside for a stroll among the stumps.

When I watch a program I like to read the credits. I like to see just who is responsible for doing what. The stars sometimes walk through their lines with the emotion of leftover potatoes, while the supporting actors and actresses do memorable work. At other times the script is hot, or the photography; the beginnings of the stars of today often lie buried in the credits of late-night movies watched by insomniacs and people getting off swing shift.

At the end of this program, the runners of errands and makers of coffee got their due, and the producers gave various thank-yous and acknowledgments. The U.S. Fish and Wildlife Service was thanked, and the U.S. Forest Service and so on. The Gifford Pinchot National Forest was in there.

'Did you see that?' Donna blinked.

'I saw it.'

Kenny O'Callahan was listed as a bird trainer to the documentary's brilliant photographer — the conniving baldie, Adonis Northlake.

29

The Sins of Bert Starkey

The next morning I called Sheriff Bert Starkey at his office in Sixkiller and arranged an early afternoon appointment with him at Minnie's. I went by myself. It was nitty-gritty time.

The sheriff knew from the fact that I had called for an appointment that I was there on serious business.

We leaned back in our chairs so the waitress could pour us cups of coffee. I could see it in his eyes that he knew he was about to confront the truth, whether he liked it or not; he himself had seen the same look in countless criminals' eyes as he had read them their rights.

Caught.

His stomach turned to sugar — this too was in his eyes. He stirred coffee and glanced about Minnie's. Was he about to trade this for a stretch in Walla Walla?

He cleared his throat softly. 'So what is it you would like to talk about that you think is so important, Mr. Denson?'

'Jenny MacIvar's murder, for one thing.'

He blinked.

'The television people say you don't have a clue. Is that really true, Sheriff? You don't have the foggiest idea what happened to her? Can't find a motive or suspect anywhere?'

'If we called the television people every time we smelled a suspicious fart, we'd never catch a crook.'

'I bet I've found out more than you have, Sheriff.'

'About the murder?' He looked surprised.

'I think I know who killed Ms. MacIvar and at least part of the motive. By the way, what do you think is the most important to the voters, a sheriff who looks good on billboards, or one who's competent?'

'If I were you, I'd tell me what you know and tell me fast, Mr. Denson. There are laws against withholding evidence.'

'In due time, Sheriff. Not so fast,' I said. I had the good hand, not Starkey. Let him suffer a bit, the son of a bitch. 'I've been going here and there, asking questions for my employer, Mr. Boogie Dewlapp. You know, routine stuff, but a pretty shocking story emerges, if you don't mind my saying so.'

'I bet,' Starkey said dryly.

'Including one little episode that gives you a motive for the murder. Took me a while to figure it out.'

'What? Murder? Me? You must be out of your mind!'

'At a minimum, I find it difficult to believe the voters would take kindly to a sheriff growing pot, then pinning the blame on an innocent couple.'

Starkey paled.

'So what do you say that just for the hell of it, I tell you what I've figured out, Sheriff? This'll be for funsies now.'

Starkey studied his fingernails. 'Funsies?'

'That's as good a name for it as any. Funsies or realsies, depending. Sheriff, I'm far more interested in justice for a case of homicide than I am in busting someone for growing cannabis. Suppose I turn my cards faceup so you can see what I've got. If you can beat 'em with the truth, fair enough. If not, we talk. That's what I mean by funsies. Pretend stuff for starters.'

He looked up at me, his eyes steady.

'If you listen to my funsies story, Sheriff, you should be able to see why logic would, as the lawyers say, compel a disinterested observer to include you among the murder suspects. Mind you, that doesn't mean you did it, or even that I necessarily think you did, but if everything I've learned were made public it would almost surely result in an untoward fuss. I'll start with pot and work up to murder, more dramatic that way.'

'I see.'

'But this is for funsies, remember.'

The sheriff chewed on a fingernail, buying a little time while he considered the pitfalls of the conversation. I didn't blame him; I would have too if I'd been in his shoes. 'Okay, I'm game. Tell me your funsies story, Mr. Denson.'

'Well, see, there's this essentially straight-arrow sheriff who gets led astray by all the easy money to be had in drugs. He's facing reelection, and that's expensive as hell. So he grows himself a patch of marijuana on the side. This is virtually risk free, since he's not about to bust himself. The only problem is that he's not very good at it, and the plants don't amount to much, possibly because there's not enough sun in Skamania County for them to mature properly. Perhaps if he had given his plants a head start under grow lights they'd have had time to do their thing.'

Starkey's compressed lips turned pale.

'Anyway, by the first week of October he's running comfortably in the polls. He can do without the money for the pathetic plants, but he has to get rid of them somehow. So he orders his deputies to begin planning a marijuana sweep between Calamity and Sixkiller. On the North Fork of Jumpoff Joe there happens to be an abandoned shack — perfect to plant the drying evidence, because nobody gets hurt in the bust. Does this all make sense so far, Sheriff?'

'I'm interested in all such theories. It's part of the job, Mr. Denson.'

'But dammit, when he's in the process of hanging the pot up in the abandoned shack he's seen by a government scientist on her way to scout spotted owl nests. Or maybe she didn't see him. He's not sure, so he moves the pot to an abandoned shack on the South Fork. There's a house down the creek apiece, but its windows are boarded over, and he concludes that it's abandoned.

'But aw shit, when his deputies make the long-planned bust, they drag in a mill worker and his wife who had been away on vacation. The sheriff doesn't know what the hell to do, poor fucker.'

'Just what would you do if you were the sheriff in this funsies story of yours, Mr. Denson?'

'I just don't know. It's a tough one. Unfortunately for the sheriff, there are complications. First, the witness tells a friend what she has seen, and this friend's having an affair with the sheriff's environmentalist brother.

'There are ways for the sheriff to see to it covertly that the innocent couple doesn't go to jail, but before he can do anything, some asshole murders the witness! Her friend doesn't know what to think and demands that the brother confront the sheriff. The sheriff may be the murderer. If something isn't done, the friend will take her case to me, a private investigator she met in Delbert's Awful Onion.

'The brother goes to see the sheriff and says something's gotta be done, bro, or they're going to have you up on a murder rap.' I paused.

'Now, the private eye goes out to the North Fork shack and makes Warrenton molds that suggest strongly that my little scenario is precisely what happened. As a matter of fact, this sheriff was wearing shoes identical to the ones you're wearing right now.'

Starkey looked at his feet, then back up at me.

'The sheriff is you. The innocent couple is Terry and Mary Ellen Harkenrider. The witness is Jenny MacIvar. The friend and confidant is Dr. Lois Angleton. The brother is Dr. Eric Starkey. The private detective is me. And on top of that, Sheriff, I happen to have known that woman — '

'Jenny MacIvar?'

' — and I know very well she wouldn't have acted on what she had seen if the innocent couple was taken off the hook. Now you strike me as a practical man. Why murder her?'

The sheriff closed his eyes. 'No reason at all. None. Zero.'

'The murder has you stumped, doesn't it, Sheriff? You know she's been living with Adonis Northlake for the last year, don't you? I bet you don't know that he is married to one Elise Paxton Northlake, heiress to a microchip fortune.'

'What?'

'Or that, nine years ago, in her name, they bought the timber rights to thousands of acres of Gifford Pinchot in this area.'

Sheriff Starkey's eyes widened. 'Well, by God, Boogie Dewlapp does hire good people, doesn't he? I had this friend back

331

in the army, a Tennesseean. He had this expression 'good on you.' Well, I say 'good on you,' Mr. Denson.'

'Of course you'd have tumbled onto that by yourself on the by-and-by, eh, Sheriff? Now you owe me one. A couple, as a matter of fact.'

Starkey braked his enthusiasm. 'Just what is it you're after, Mr. Denson? Aside from the dropping of charges against the Harkenriders, which I can arrange, and a close, hard look at Adonis Northlake, which I can assure you I will take pronto.' He looked as if he had something more he wanted to say but thought better of it.

'Sheriff, I came up here last week because of the Harkenrider case. Then Jenny MacIvar was murdered, and that meant a second case, because she was a friend of mine. Then I got a third case.'

'Which was?'

'To find out who wrung the neck of the spotted owl that was stolen from the Hog Wild Saloon.'

'What?'

'As it happens, I could use a little help with that one.'

Starkey hesitated. 'Of course, I'll do anything I can to help you out.'

'Ahh, good.'

He added quickly, 'Within reason, Mr. Denson. You have to remember I have an election coming up next week.'

'Sheriff, I was smart enough to figure out whose pot that was on the Harkenriders' place, and I delivered you Jenny MacIvar's likely murderer. If I'm right, Bosley Ellin and Adonis Northlake — with the help of Kenny O'Callahan — moved a bunch of spotted owls from northern California to Sixkiller in a scheme to get a favorable owl count in Gifford Pinchot. They could have flown the owls up or driven them up on the Interstate. No problem.'

'They what?'

'In order to release the owls most effectively, they needed to know, in advance, specific tracts of timber where the ornithologists would count birds. Northlake got that advance information from Jenny MacIvar — until she found out about his wife.'

'Oh, boy. Maybe she found out about the owls, too.'

'She could have, although that's hard to tell.' I wondered: Had Adonis Northlake conned his way into Jenny's bed and heart solely because she counted spotted owls? Is that what had happened? Is that what Jenny learned about the perfect one? 'Sheriff, I want to go on a war party tonight with my partner and his friends. We'll need you to look the other way when we're on our way out of there, traveling fast.'

'By 'war party' you mean?'

'I mean get those owls the hell away from Gifford Pinchot. I think they're being kept at Ellin's retreat up the North Fork.'

'At Ellin's place?' Bosley Ellin was a Mr. Big in Skamania County, and the sheriff, despite the jam he was in, remained a political animal. 'Are you sure there isn't some other way? I'm not so sure I want to . . . ' Starkey glanced about as though looking for help, from whom I wasn't sure. His wife? The Beneficent Sheriffs' Association? His dog?

'I can still call the media people if you want. No problem.' Starkey hadn't cared that the Harkenriders suffered, so I didn't give squat about him.

His face tightened. *He* was the public's designated bully. *He* was the one who pushed his weight around, not other people. He didn't like being on the receiving end. Not one bit. It galled him, but there was nothing he could do.

'Well? It's your choice,' I said.

'I can do it, I guess.'

''I guess'? When your picture's in the paper as a pot grower and murder suspect, you'll have pouches again and very little hair. Now there's something for you to think about, Sheriff. Under the circumstances, surely you can be more decisive than an 'I guess.' I bet your mama taught you to be more pragmatic than that.'

I'd figured everything out. Now, Starkey's badge meant bullshit. His career was on the line. He grimaced. He was defeated. 'All right, I'll do it.' He clenched his jaw. He glanced at his watch. 'Give me a call before you push off. You should avoid the interstate highway. If you drive east through the mountains and come down at Stevenson, you'll be in Skamania County all the way. You can cross the Columbia into Oregon on the Bridge of the Gods. I can't help you in Cowlitz County.'

'Cross over the Columbia at the Bridge of the Gods, you're saying?'

'That's the way I'd do it. Do you know how to find Ellin's hideout?'

'Not exactly. It's up past the hot springs.'

Starkey took a pad out and drew me a map as he talked. 'You take the first left past the hot springs, then you go two miles and watch on your right for a turnoff marked by a couple of 'no trespassing' signs. There's a guard shack around the first bend of the road into his place, about a hundred yards or so in. The first thing I'd do is I'd hide my rig somewhere and scout the place out.'

'I was told he has a barn out there where he stores his vintage cars.'

'Yes, he does, back in the trees to the rear of his house.'

'I'm betting that's where he's keeping the owls. Much obliged, Sheriff. I mean it.'

Starkey took a deep breath and released it slowly. 'Mr. Denson, I have a question for you, a sincere one, although under the present circumstances you may think it a form of plea bargaining. As a private citizen, which would you rather have me do as an elected sheriff: accept money from an individual or corporation or committee to whom or to which I would be indebted, or try my hand at growing marijuana? We're not talking cocaine here, we're talking pot.'

I didn't say anything.

'You want to know what burns my ass, Denson?'

I shrugged.

He held his hand palm-down about a yard from the floor. 'A flame about that high.'

30

The Making of Flaming Arrows

We didn't want to drive south with owls crapping on our shoulders or trying to perch on the steering wheel, so we used two of Little Eagle Brown's salmon nets to block off the front seats of my minibus and his old Chevrolet van.

Donna Cowapoo rode with me, followed by the bread van carrying the main war party: Willie Prettybird, Melvin, Duke, Toro, and Little Eagle Brown. The van had once been used to deliver Wonder bread, and the side panels featured a faded portrait of a rosy-cheeked little girl with blond ringlets eating a slice of bread and butter.

I wheeled my bus in and out of the tight curves of the mountain road, gearing from second to third and back, the air-cooled engine humming steady and true. In my rearview mirror I could see

Little Eagle leaning forward, determinedly steering his van into action as though it were an Appaloosa pony bearing down on John Wayne. He was Little Eagle Brown, warrior, going into battle.

If the Indians had been suppressed and scattered with the coming of the Europeans, tonight Willie and his war party — with Donna Cowapoo and a blundering paleface at their side — would strike back in the manner of their aggrieved ancestors.

Old-growth Douglas firs and spotted owls were in the territory of tweenies; maybe the public would buy them as indispensable to the future, maybe not. At best they were a hard sell for the Sierra Club and the Audubon Society.

I may have been stupidly romantic and too easily persuaded by accounts of the importance of trees to the environment and the quality of life, but I was on the side of the old-growth forest.

Following Sheriff Starkey's instructions, we came at last to the two yellow signs that signaled the road to Ellin's retreat. One said PRIVATE PROPERTY, DEAD END, and the other a simple NO TRESPASSING. There are frivolous signs, signs tacked up on the half-baked advice of barroom lawyers, signs clearly erected because everybody else has one and the owner feels insecure without one, and dead-on serious signs. These particular signs signaled a clear message to Skamanian passers-by: The owner of this property was hard-core about wanting people to stay the hell out.

I went on by, looking for a place where we could discuss our operation in private. After another half mile, I spotted an abandoned road on the right, leading north into the forest — two graveled ruts with a median of weeds. I turned the bus around, and Donna parted the owl nets and scrambled to the rear window to help me out as I backed down the ruts, weeds scraping the bottom of my bus. The trees and underbrush blocked the view of the road after fifty yards, and I stopped the bus.

Little Eagle Brown did the same with his bread truck, and Donna and I got out and went forward to join them. With Willie leading the discussion, we decided that Little Eagle would scout Ellin's estate; Willie would circle the guard shack and see if there was a guard on duty.

Little Eagle hopped neatly to the rear of the van and pulled a bow and a quiver of arrows from the gear he had assembled; he slipped the quiver over his shoulder and disappeared north into the forest in the direction of the lake and Ellin's house. Willie headed east, back toward the Boz's road where Starkey said the guardhouse stood.

It was cold in the bread truck, and Donna Cowapoo leaned next to me for warmth and snuggled her head in the hollow of my shoulder. We waited in silence.

Ten minutes later we heard a ferocious barking that continued for a nerve-racking half minute before it suddenly stopped.

'Did he eliminate the dog?' I asked Melvin.

'If he had to.'

Twenty minutes later we heard a

rustling outside and Little Eagle Brown was at the door. He blew on his cupped hands for a moment to warm them up, then said:

'First thing I had to do was take out the fucking dog. A barker. The owls are there.'

'Where?' I said.

Little Eagle put a finger to his lips and a hand to one ear. 'Willie's coming.'

In a few seconds, Willie arrived — soundlessly to me. I don't know how Little Eagle was able to hear him.

'They're there, Willie,' he said.

'Good,' said Willie. 'We lucked out with the security shack. No guard tonight. I could see a log bridge down the road. What did you find out?'

Little Eagle said, 'The bridge crosses the creek that empties out of Ellin's private lake on the west; it's not a big lake, maybe twenty yards wide and maybe fifty or sixty yards long. The road forks on the other side of the bridge. Left to the house on the north shore of the lake; right to the barn set back in the trees — say twenty yards northeast of the house.

Maybe Ellin used to store his restored cars there, but not now.'

'Security?' said Willie.

'There's a chain-link fence around the barn, which I went right over. The windows are shuttered, but I was still able to get a peek inside. We can take the hasp on the lock to the gate with boltcutters and back the bus and van to the front door. No problem with the door.'

'How many owls?'

'Thirty or forty, maybe as many as fifty or sixty; it's hard to tell. They've got perches everywhere. Incidentally, Bosley Ellin, Adonis Northlake, and Kenny O'Callahan are all in the house. They're having a big powwow of some kind in the living room. There's a picture window that overlooks the lake. You can see them clearly from this side of the water.'

'Are they calm or arguing?'

'Quarreling. Northlake and Ellin mostly. Getting damned hot at times. The logger doesn't appear to be saying much.'

Willie turned to me. 'What do you think, Denson?'

'I think Ellin probably got rid of his

guard when he moved his cars out. He wanted privacy when they brought the owls in. I say they're figuring where they can move the birds temporarily.'

Willie gnawed on the nail of his forefinger. 'The question is: can we get the owls out?'

Little Eagle leaned forward. 'If we figure it right.'

Willie turned to me. 'Denson?'

'I say we need a diversion of some kind. Who knows what kind of shotguns and hunting rifles they might have in there?'

Little Eagle said, 'Suppose I launch some fire arrows at his house. I can loop them across the lake. That ought to divert him, don't you think? He was willing to cut down the last of our big trees. I don't feel guilty about burning a few of his fancy shingles.'

Willie grinned. 'Fire arrows. I love it. But fire arrows made from what?'

Little Eagle shrugged. 'From our underwear. We'll siphon ourselves some gas. Everybody donates his shorts. We'll cut 'em up and wrap 'em and soak 'em.'

Willie said, 'Okay. Now. How about if I

take Donna and Denson and Melvin to the owl barn and Duke and Toro stay back to drive the bus and van. Duke? Toro?'

'Fine by me,' Duke said.

Toro scratched his gut by way of agreement.

'Little Eagle, you wait on the near shore and watch them through the picture window.'

'You'll need bolt cutters for the fence gate, Willie.'

'We've got 'em.' Willie said. 'When we're ready to move owls, we'll give you some coyote yelps. When you hear the yelps, Duke, you and Toro start your engines.'

'Got it,' Toro said.

Little Eagle said, 'If they get spooked inside the house, I'll give you a panther scream and start launching fire arrows from across the lake. I might not be able to burn the house down, but I'll sure as hell hold their attention.'

Willie said, 'We've got some fire arrows to make. Let's do it then.'

We piled outside in the cold to

contribute our underwear for Little Eagle's fire arrows. Eyes up out of respect for Donna, we dropped our trousers in the frigid air and skinned off our shorts, laughing and fumbling with shoelaces and zippers and buttons.

Unfortunately, the only paleface in the war party, the private detective who refused to carry a weapon, had chosen to wear his favorite boxer shorts, those featuring a smoking revolver on the front with a long, Texas buntline barrel of outsized proportions.

There was nothing I could do except get my pants and shoes back on as quickly as possible and stand there grinning while Willie and Little Eagle and Donna and their pals risked warning Bosley Ellin with their burst of laughter.

Then we jumped back into the warmth of the bread truck and set about cutting and ripping the underwear into ribbons.

31

War Party

Little Eagle Brown took point, by consensus; he had scouted the territory, and he knew the pitfalls. Little Eagle was young and had good eyes, and judging from his obvious skill at following trails by the light of the moon, he was both athletic and intelligent.

Willie Prettybird, who was high on the pecking order of the raiding party and carried bolt cutters and a crowbar, led the way after Little Eagle Brown. Little Eagle had wire cutters in his hip pocket and a quiver of fire arrows slung over his shoulder. The earnest Melvin, whose advice Willie obviously respected, followed close on Prettybird's heels. Then Donna.

I was fifth in the line.

We moved in single file through the gloom of forest in the direction of the road.

When my turn came I wanted to stand in there like Gary Cooper, but I knew we were all at the mercy of the screw-up god. The fear that the Great Lord of Fuck-ups almost certainly lay waiting in ambush kept me dry-mouthed and on the balls of my feet.

Ten minutes later Little Eagle Brown stopped, and Willie, Melvin, Donna, and I gathered around him. We could see the lights of the house through the under-brush — including, even at our angle, the figures behind the huge window that faced the lake. Moonlight reflected off the water, and the profile of the trees on the western shore was etched into a silver mirror.

Backs low, we passed quickly over the bridge.

Willie led Melvin, Donna, and me to the right in the direction of the barn where Ellin had once kept his restored automobiles. Moments later, we were there. The barn was maybe forty feet wide and eighty feet long; large portions of the high, curved roof were glass skylights.

Without ado, Willie cut open the gate

to the chain-link fence and hurried inside, dropping to his knees with his crowbar at the front door. It took him about two minutes to open it.

I had my back to Willie when he went into his yelping routine.

Did Little Eagle have enough time to nip the phone wires and hustle around to the far side of the lake?

From across the water, a single yelp in return. Little Eagle was ready.

We waited, and moments later heard the loping of my VW engine. The engines grew louder, and I could see the bus and bread truck crossing the bridge with their lights out.

Then, on the far side of the lake, the scream of a panther.

It was a clear night. Someone inside the house had no doubt seen the vehicles as they crossed the bridge.

A shooting star of flame arched through the blackness from the far shore and hit the roof of Bosley Ellin's house with an audible thud. A second flaming arrow looped toward the house.

On the far side of the house, a door

slammed. A man who had obviously stepped outside yelled, 'Jesus Christ! Fucking arrows!'

'What?' another man yelled.

Another flaming arrow hit the roof with a thud. Little Eagle Brown had moved down the creek.

'Indians! An attack by goddamn Indians!' the first one yelled. 'That one's spreading, get a hose.'

Duke and Toro turned the bus and the bread truck around and backed down the road to the open gate in the fence.

Willie said, 'Denson, you'll drive on the way out. In your bus, please. If you have to go, then go. We'll get as many owls as we can. You stay with the van, please, Duke.'

Duke and I did as we were told. Willie, Donna, Melvin, and Toro went inside and emerged clutching an owl in each hand. Moments later, the rear door of my bus opened, and Donna Cowapoo gently tossed a spotted owl inside, followed by a second. The owls looked up at me and blinked, but didn't seem particularly alarmed.

Willie was right behind Donna with two more owls.

I heard the crack of a high-powered rifle and held my breath momentarily.

Another arrow shot out of the darkness; this one crashed through glass. No rifle shot came; there was now much swearing and yelling for water inside the house.

Willie and Donna made another owl trip, then another and another until the floor of my bus was a clutter of large-eyed, blinking birds. They seemed remarkably unconcerned or resigned to their fate.

Donna Cowapoo hopped inside. Then Willie, standing at my ear, gave another coyote yelp and slapped the door of my bus.

'Go for it, Kemosabe,' he said.

I did as I was told. Smoke poured from the windows of Bosley Ellin's hideaway.

A grinning Little Eagle Brown was waiting on the far side of the bridge, waving me past.

In the rearview mirror I watched as Little Eagle grabbed a can from Melvin and sloshed something onto the log bridge, then hopped aboard the bread truck as behind him, the bridge burst into flames.

We were a half mile down Jumpoff Joe Creek before we met the flashing red lights of a fire truck that whooshed by going *aaaaawwwweeeeeoooooo*.

A couple of minutes later, while we were still a mile shy of the intersection at the Lucky Buck, we found a squad car with flashing blue lights turned sideways in the road, blocking the way. We stopped.

Sheriff Bert T. Starkey got out of the squad car.

Donna jerked her head back toward the bread truck. 'What do we do now?'

'We let the paleface take care of it.'

Starkey got close. I saw that his brother Eric was sitting in the car. I rolled down the window.

Starkey said, 'Well, we got a call from Bosley Ellin . . . ' Then he saw the owls in the back of the minibus. He waved his brother out of the car. 'You have to see this, Eric.'

The man from the Audubon Society

got out of the car and peered through the window at the owls. 'I have to go. Have to. Did you ask him?'

Starkey turned pale. 'I had to tell Eric about all this, of course. He wants to know if he can go with you, Mr. Denson.'

'What?' I looked at Eric. Then I hopped out of the bus, and I went back to the van. Willie had taken the wheel from Duke.

'We got the sheriff's brother, the Audubon Society guy, who wants to go with us.'

'Shit, Denson!'

'Thanks, Willie.' I turned and ran back to the minibus. 'You'll have to sit on the toolbox between Donna and me.'

Eric hopped up and onto the toolbox without a word.

At my shoulder, the sheriff said, 'I have to put in an appearance at the fire, and then I'll catch up.'

I waited for a moment while the sheriff got into his car and drove off toward Ellin's. Eric Starkey turned on my toolbox, wide-eyed at the spotted owls in the back.

He said, 'How many are there?'

Donna said, 'Eighteen owls in each truck.'

I said, 'Plus a war party of five redskins in the bread truck.'

He said, 'I just had to go. I wanted to be able to say later that I was there.'

I put the bus in gear, and, driving fast and then some, our two-vehicle caravan was off to Calamity, the first leg of the road through the Cascade Mountains.

A half hour later, a squad car from Skamania County fishtailed out of a side road and bore down on us, blue lights flashing, then just as quickly pulled to the side of the road. Sheriff Bert Starkey on the job. So far, so good.

I put pedal to the floor and pushed my bus hard through the tight curves. Behind me, eighteen sets of huge eyes watched the action through the fishnet.

32

On the Bridge of the Gods

According to stories passed down by the tribes of the Pacific Northwest and confirmed by geologists, the gorge where the Columbia River cuts through the Cascade Mountains was once spanned by a natural land bridge. The Indians call this the Bridge of the Gods.

In 1936, the federal government built the Bonneville Dam across the Columbia at a point where the great arch possibly once stood. Less than a mile downstream from the dam, they built a steel bridge they called the Bridge of the Gods.

We were heading for it. The clear night had given way to a gloom of rain as we drove east from Calamity up fifty miles of winding mountain highway through the Gifford Pinchot.

The first subtle hints of warmth began to appear in the east as Sheriff Starkey caught up with us ten miles short of the Columbia River and pulled us over with a flashing blue light. Starkey piled out of his car and ran toward my bus, his belly bouncing.

Willie did the same.

Breathing hard from the effort, Starkey said, 'About twenty miles back, one of my deputies called dispatch with the license numbers of your bus and van saying you were speeding, and he was giving chase. I don't know if you saw him or not.'

'We saw him,' I said.

'I called him off, saying I'd take care of it. A few minutes ago, I called dispatch and said I was still giving chase and asked had there been any inquiries about the two vehicles. I was told yes, there had been.'

'Ellin?'

'That's my bet. If it was, he knows where you're headed.'

Willie said, 'Let's get moving, then.' He turned and sprinted back to the van.

The edge of the sun was just shy of the cloudless horizon when we turned west along the Columbia for the short run to the bridge.

The rising sun, a bright cauldron, reflected reddish orange on everything in the gorge: the water, the trees, the girders of the Bridge of the Gods. The two-lane suspension bridge, nearly sixty feet above the water, had recently been painted white, and the effect was little short of electrifying, as though the bridge were on fire.

The sheriff led us to the entrance of the bridge, then pulled to the side of the road and gave us a wave as he headed for home.

I was three quarters of the way across, the blinding sun on my left, when a Toyota four-wheeler pulled out to pass Willie's bread van behind me. I heard the dull thump of an explosion.

In my rearview mirror, I saw the van lurch toward the center of the bridge.

Before I could react, the Toyota was alongside me.

I caught a glimpse of Adonis Northlake a fraction of a second before *boom! boom!* his shotgun took my left front tire.

Northlake barreled around me and skidded dangerously to a halt, blocking both lanes.

Behind me, Willie, honking his horn, put his bread truck into a hard retreat.

I did the same, struggling to control the bucking steering wheel, until *boom, boom*, I took a blast in my right front tire and one straight into the right headlight.

With both front tires flat and a lunatic with a shotgun pointed at me, I stopped.

Behind me, Willie did the same.

'Back, back, back with the owls,' I told Donna and Eric.

I followed them through the fishnet, and we squatted at the rear of the bus, blinking owls looking up at us. A shotgun blast caught the left top of my windshield, sending pellets of shatterproof glass ripping into the roof.

In front of us, Adonis Northlake crouched behind his Toyota with a shotgun. As far as I knew, we had just one weapon, Little Eagle Brown's bow and arrow.

Northlake shouted, 'Denson!'

The windshield shattered from another

direct hit, pellets of glass lashing me on my left cheek and temple.

I dove for the floor, the side of my face stinging.

Donna and Eric took the pellets on the back of their heads and necks.

I scooted on the floor to the front of the bus, leaned over, and swung the door open to see what would happen. It took a shotgun blast. I scrambled quickly back.

'Out the back,' I said. I followed Donna's jeaned rump through the rear door, where Little Eagle Brown waited with his bow and quiver of arrows.

Willie, with Melvin looking over his shoulder, watched from the front seat of the bread van.

Little Eagle said, 'We'll need to know which way Northlake's coming. Listen to Willie. One yelp he's on our right, two on our left.'

'Where are Duke and Toro?'

'On the underside of these girders, seeing if they can work their way behind Northlake for an ambush.'

From in front of us, Northlake shouted, 'All I want're the owls, Denson.'

I shouted back: 'Where are Bosley and Kenny?'

'Back with the fire. I want those owls.'

I said, 'All we want is for you to get out of our way.'

Northlake said, 'Unless you want to load up on buckshot, you'd better do as I say and put those pieces of shit you call vehicles into slow and easy reverse. I know you're driving on flats, but you can do it.'

'We need to talk it over,' I called. 'You'll have to give us a couple of minutes.'

'You want to try taking me on with a bow and arrow?'

'You want to tell us how it felt to murder the woman you lived with for more than a year?'

'I want those owls.'

'Would you like to tell us how Jenny learned that the wonderful photographer Adonis Northlake, lover of kids and old ladies, was a chickenshit speculator and hypocrite on the grand scale? All the while married to a rich woman in Chicago. And still, there you were, chasing money like a hound after rabbits.

Did Jenny find out about your wife? Is that what happened, Adonis? Is that why you murdered her? Couldn't disappoint Elise?'

'I murdered her out of simple perspective, Denson. Common sense. People want to build houses, but they don't want to cut down trees. We're talking the northern variety of the spotted owls here, not all spotted owls. We're talking hundreds of millions of dollars and tens of thousands of jobs, but what happens? We boo-hoo over owls that nobody ever sees anyway.'

He waited for me to say something, but I kept my mouth shut. I wanted him to keep talking, and he did.

'Did it matter that I was married? Jenny was happy. Elise was happy. The rest is sentimental shit. Big fucking deal. Hey, there comes a point and it's too much. You know, Denson, I'd like to take this shotgun and shove it up that self-righteous ass of yours and pump off two or three rounds. How would you like that, Mr. Private Detective?'

I didn't think I would like it.

'Two of them. I had to listen to two women at once, can you imagine? One in Chicago, a multimillionaire believer in astrology and reincarnation, nagging me to cut that damned timber. Another in Portland who's bonkers over vegetables and birds. I had to get rid of one of them. Which one would you choose?'

In falsetto, Northlake yelled, 'Just look at those cute, cute owls. Those great big eyes! My heavens, we can't let those awful meanies kill the habitat of our precious spotted owls.'

He dropped the falsetto. Here was a guy with thunderstorms in his cortex; the synapses could not hold, and mere anarchy was loosed in his brain.

Then, just as fast, he calmed down. 'There came a point when I said no. A point where I'd had enough. No more. I said Jenny, use your head, woman. Common sense has to rule. But no. Slapped me. What else could I do? I didn't have any choice but to blast her. Bitch.'

She had slapped him and loosed demons.

He tilted into yet another zone, and fell into a vicious chant, spitting out b's like bullets: 'Bitches and blasters. Bitches and blasters. Blast her, blast her, blast her. Bitches and blasters. Bitches and blood. Bitches and blasters and bodies and blood. Blast her. Blast her. Blast her. Evil fucking bitches. That's what old Bill Shakespeare said, wasn't it? Or was it Charles Bukowski? Or Richard Speck?'

'Why did you wring the neck of that spotted owl?'

'Oh, isn't that sweet? Posturing for a sweet little squaw, are we?' He made loud kissing sounds with his lips. Big smackers.

'Why did you?'

'Because it crapped on the back of my hand!'

'What?'

Northlake seemed surprised that I could ask such a question. 'Sure. I was in a mood where I don't take shit from anybody, much less an owl. A bird craps on my hand, then it gets its fucking neck wrung. It's as simple as that. Jenny slapped my face. Owl crapped on my hand. Same result, both times.

'Also, Denson, I happen to know you don't even carry a weapon. Jenny thought that was oh-so-wonderful! Anything to get pussy, eh, Denson? Posturing son of a bitch. See what that old nobility crapola gets you. I've got a blaster, and you've got shit.'

I said to Little Eagle Brown and Donna, 'I say we turn the owls loose. Why not?'

Donna said, 'We're closer to Oregon than Washington. They'll head there. And we're far enough away that even if they don't, they won't be part of the count.'

Little Eagle said, 'This is as good a place as any.'

'I want my owls back now, dammit, or I'm gonna show you how to use a shotgun.' Northlake's voice had edged toward the territory of sanity. Then something snapped upstairs. 'Sons-a-bitches. Sons-a-bitches.' Another chant was growing. The electricity was popping. 'Sons-a-bitches. Sons-a-bitches,' he said, increasing the pace, developing a rhythm that was not unlike a steam engine warming up. Slow at first, then faster, faster.

Donna said, 'Well, we can't give him a lobotomy, and I'm tired of listening to him.' She opened the rear door of the bus and grabbed an owl. She pitched it into the air.

'Hey!' Adonis yelled.

She threw another owl. And another.

In the van behind us, Willie yelped twice, waving with his hand.

We dove to our right around the end of the bus . . .

. . . Northlake's shotgun exploded twice, once at us, once at Willie.

Little Eagle, the last to dive for cover, got hit in the calf of his leg, which was a mass of blood.

'I'm okay,' Willie yelled. He was now doing his spying from the rear of the van, sticking his head around the corner.

I grabbed Little Eagle's bow and quiver of arrows and fumbled, trying to notch an arrow.

I drew it nearly to the point, aiming it chest high at the corner of the bus.

But Northlake didn't come. He had backed off.

Little Eagle winced as Donna ripped

back the bloody bottom of his jeans.

'I'll have to make a tourniquet,' she said.

Willie yelped three times and repeated the call.

Little Eagle said, 'Three means he's on the other side.' He gave Donna a pocketknife to help her with her work.

I nodded. I understood. I repeated the calls to myself so I wouldn't screw up. One yelp and he was coming from our right. Two and he was coming from our left.

This was to be Indian style. Listen to Willie. Be patient.

Duke and Toro were somewhere on the underside of the bridge, inching their way toward Oregon.

Three yelps.

Northlake was opposite us on the upstream side of the bus, the rising sun at his back.

A shotgun blast. At Willie, not us.

Three yelps.

Northlake was still opposite us.

I eased back on the bow.

Silence.

I waited, arrow notched. I wet my lips. Show time.

One yelp.

I faced the Oregon side, arrow drawn.

Nothing.

I waited.

Three yelps again; Northlake had retreated to the far side.

I relaxed.

Let Willie tell me.

Wait for Duke and Toro.

Patience.

Indian Style.

Two yelps. Northlake was on the Washington side of the bus.

My mouth was dry. My wrist did not tremble. The pull of the bow was nothing. I was juiced, yet calm.

Two more yelps. Crap!

Happened fast.

There he was with his shotgun . . .

. . . and there was Toro, rushing him from the side of the bridge . . .

. . . as I released the arrow.

It hit Northlake straight in the center of his torso, nearly square in the heart. I could hardly have missed. He wasn't more than a yard away.

He dropped his shotgun.

He blinked. Toro's well-timed rush had distracted him, or he'd have killed me.

He lurched to the rail of the bridge and clung to it with his elbow.

He looked down at the arrow sticking through him. He looked at me, mouth open. His elbow slipped off the rail. He dropped to his knees.

I suppose I could have done something for him, perhaps try to remove the arrow, but I wasn't in a generous mood. Instead, I shouted in his face, enunciating every word as clearly as I could so that the words would reverberate through his ebbing consciousness:

'The reason the forests are being destroyed and the owls are being killed is the same reason the Aztecs were slaughtered and the Cherokees displaced and Chief Joseph run to ground and the Columbia River chopped up by hydroelectric dams from here to the Canadian border. Greed. The notion that a man's worth is measured by what he drives or what he wears. How much is enough,

Northlake? How much?

'You don't think I know Jenny? You don't think she hurt? How about this little item? Ask yourself under what circumstances I come to know something like this: If Jenny told you once, she told you ten thousand times, you miserable son of a bitch! Do not turn the heat up so goddamn high when you cook eggs!'

His mouth moved.

'Hard to get pissed with an arrow sticking through you, is it?'

He struggled but could say nothing.

'You turned the heat full blast every damned time. The same way with the trees. You and your wife owned cutting rights to some timber in the Gifford Pinchot, so by God you were going to cut it. To hell with the owls and the public. Had to cut it now. Couldn't wait. Didn't make a fuck what it took. Look at where impatience got you. Impatience and tantrums. Just look.'

Northlake said, 'I . . . '

I'd given Jenny MacIvar the last word. All Adonis could do was open his mouth and make odd sounds.

369

I wasn't finished. I flat-out spit in his face. Landed a wad right between his eyes. 'Kenny and the Boz were at least defending a way of life. You weren't defending anything except your wallet, you contemptible bastard. Where's the honor there? What good will that timber do you when you're dead? Huh? What good? I ought to take that fucking shotgun of yours and blow your balls off.'

He opened his mouth, then toppled over, every bit as dead as Jenny MacIvar was when Starkey's deputies pulled her from the Lewis River.

The orange of the sun now completely filled the gorge.

Donna and I and Willie, joined by Melvin and Toro and Duke and Eric Starkey, set about stopping the bleeding of Little Eagle Brown's leg.

We breathed out hearty clouds of white as, one by one, we gave the remaining spotted owls a good-bye squeeze of support and affection and pitched them skyward into the cold air. We watched as they turned and flew south toward Oregon.

The gorge was ablaze with color and beautiful as the last owl disappeared. Then Sheriff Starkey's siren broke the silence.

I had always refused to carry a weapon because I didn't want to have to use it. Now I had killed a man with a bow and arrow.

I had delivered for Jenny MacIvar. I had come through for Willie Prettybird and the animal people, surely the most unusual clients a private eye ever had. I had solved one for Boogie Dewlapp. I was finished with my business in Calamity, Washington.

Donna Cowapoo leaned against me as we waited.

I said, 'When the sheriff says we can go, I say we drive on down to Portland and have a sandwich at Produce Row. Maybe Phil Sanford will come over, and we can tell him a story.'

'Sure,' she said.

I held Donna tightly, remembering the time I heard panthers purring in the night.

We do hope that you have enjoyed reading this large print book.

Did you know that all of our titles are available for purchase?

We publish a wide range of high quality large print books including:
Romances, Mysteries, Classics
General Fiction
Non Fiction and Westerns

Special interest titles available in large print are:
The Little Oxford Dictionary
Music Book, Song Book
Hymn Book, Service Book

Also available from us courtesy of Oxford University Press:
Young Readers' Dictionary
(large print edition)
Young Readers' Thesaurus
(large print edition)

For further information or a free brochure, please contact us at:
Ulverscroft Large Print Books Ltd.,
The Green, Bradgate Road, Anstey,
Leicester, LE7 7FU, England.
Tel: (00 44) **0116 236 4325**
Fax: (00 44) **0116 234 0205**

Other titles in the
Linford Mystery Library:

CRADLE SNATCH

Peter Conway

Mr. Justice Craythorne is convinced that Janice Beaton is a wicked woman and sentences her to three years in prison — but later he is to discover just how wicked she is. After kidnapping the judge's baby grandson, she proceeds to terrorise his family . . . Cathy Weston leads the investigation but finds herself becoming emotionally involved with the baby's father. The physical and psychological pressures mount, and the young and vulnerable police inspector now finds herself targeted by Beaton and her sinister accomplice.

ODD WOMAN OUT

George Douglas

Chief Inspector Bill Hallam and sergeant 'Jack' Spratt of the Deniston C.I.D. are investigating the death of Madge Adkin. The dead woman had peculiar habits and claimed to be a bird-watcher, but knew nothing about birds. The trail they follow leads them to an escaped prisoner, an unorthodox 'healer' and a bunch of anonymous letters . . . The killer seems to have covered his tracks, but a blackmail attempt, quite unconnected with the murder, brings the detectives the proof they need.